T0144922

The Yellow Mask

The Yellow Mask

Wilkie Collins

MINT EDITIONS

The Yellow Mask was first published in 1855.

This edition published by Mint Editions 2021.

ISBN 9781513135830 | E-ISBN 9781513287218

Published by Mint Editions®

MINT
EDITIONS

minteditionbooks.com

Publishing Director: Jennifer Newens
Design & Production: Rachel Lopez Metzger
Project Manager: Micaela Clark
Typesetting: Westchester Publishing Services

Contents

PART FIRST

I

About a century ago, there lived in the ancient city of Pisa a famous Italian milliner, who, by way of vindicating to all customers her familiarity with Paris fashions, adopted a French title, and called herself the Demoiselle Grifoni. She was a wizen little woman with a mischievous face, a quick tongue, a nimble foot, a talent for business, and an uncertain disposition. Rumor hinted that she was immensely rich, and scandal suggested that she would do anything for money.

The one undeniable good quality which raised Demoiselle Grifoni above all her rivals in the trade was her inexhaustible fortitude. She was never known to yield an inch under any pressure of adverse circumstances. Thus the memorable occasion of her life on which she was threatened with ruin was also the occasion on which she most triumphantly asserted the energy and decision of her character. At the height of the demoiselle's prosperity her skilled forewoman and cutter-out basely married and started in business as her rival. Such a calamity as this would have ruined an ordinary milliner; but the invincible Grifoni rose superior to it almost without an effort, and proved incontestably that it was impossible for hostile Fortune to catch her at the end of her resources. While the minor milliners were prophesying that she would shut up shop, she was quietly carrying on a private correspondence with an agent in Paris. Nobody knew what these letters were about until a few weeks had elapsed, and then circulars were received by all the ladies in Pisa, announcing that the best French forewoman who could be got for money was engaged to superintend the great Grifoni establishment. This master-stroke decided the victory. All the demoiselle's customers declined giving orders elsewhere until the forewoman from Paris had exhibited to the natives of Pisa the latest fashions from the metropolis of the world of dress.

The Frenchwoman arrived punctual to the appointed day—glib and curt, smiling and flippant, tight of face and supple of figure. Her name was Mademoiselle Virginie, and her family had inhumanly deserted her. She was set to work the moment she was inside the doors of the Grifoni establishment. A room was devoted to her own private use; magnificent materials in velvet, silk, and satin, with due accompaniment of muslins, laces, and ribbons were placed at her disposal; she was told to spare no expense, and to produce, in the shortest possible time, the finest and nearest specimen dresses for exhibition in the show-room. Mademoiselle Virginie undertook to do everything required of her, produced her portfolios of patterns and her book of colored designs, and asked for one assistant who could speak French enough to interpret her orders to the Italian girls in the work-room.

"I have the very person you want," cried Demoiselle Grifoni. "A work-woman we call Brigida here—the idlest slut in Pisa, but as sharp as a needle—has been in France, and speaks the language like a native. I'll send her to you directly."

Mademoiselle Virginie was not left long alone with her patterns and silks. A tall woman, with bold black eyes, a reckless manner, and a step as firm as a man's, stalked into the room with the gait of a tragedy-queen crossing the stage. The instant her eyes fell on the French forewoman, she stopped, threw up her hands in astonishment, and exclaimed, "Finette!"

"Teresa!" cried the Frenchwoman, casting her scissors on the table, and advancing a few steps.

"Hush! call me Brigida."

"Hush! call me Virginie."

These two exclamations were uttered at the same moment, and then the two women scrutinized each other in silence. The swarthy cheeks of the Italian turned to a dull yellow, and the voice of the Frenchwoman trembled a little when she spoke again.

"How, in the name of Heaven, have you dropped down in the world as low as this?" she asked. "I thought you were provided for when—"

"Silence!" interrupted Brigida. "You see I was not provided for. I have had my misfortunes; and you are the last woman alive who ought to refer to them."

"Do you think I have not had my misfortunes, too, since we met?" (Brigida's face brightened maliciously at those words.) "You have had your revenge," continued Mademoiselle Virginie, coldly, turning away to the table and taking up the scissors again.

Brigida followed her, threw one arm roughly round her neck, and kissed her on the cheek. "Let us be friends again," she said. The Frenchwoman laughed. "Tell me how I have had my revenge," pursued the other, tightening her grasp. Mademoiselle Virginie signed to Brigida to stoop, and whispered rapidly in her ear. The Italian listened eagerly, with fierce, suspicious eyes fixed on the door. When the whispering ceased, she loosened her hold, and, with a sigh of relief, pushed back her heavy black hair from her temples. "Now we are friends," she said, and sat down indolently in a chair placed by the worktable.

"Friends," repeated Mademoiselle Virginie, with another laugh. "And now for business," she continued, getting a row of pins ready for use by putting them between her teeth. "I am here, I believe, for the purpose of ruining the late forewoman, who has set up in opposition to us? Good! I *will* ruin her. Spread out the yellow brocaded silk, my dear, and pin that pattern on at your end, while I pin at mine. And what are your plans, Brigida? (Mind you don't forget that Finette is dead, and that Virginie has risen from her ashes.) You can't possibly intend to stop here all your life? (Leave an inch outside the paper, all round.) You must have projects? What are they?"

"Look at my figure," said Brigida, placing herself in an attitude in the middle of the room.

"Ah," rejoined the other, "it's not what it was. There's too much of it. You want diet, walking, and a French stay-maker," muttered Mademoiselle Virginie through her chevaus-defrise of pins.

"Did the goddess Minerva walk, and employ a French stay-maker? I thought she rode upon clouds, and lived at a period before waists were invented."

"What do you mean?"

"This—that my present project is to try if I can't make my fortune by sitting as a model for Minerva in the studio of the best sculptor in Pisa."

"And who is he! (Unwind me a yard or two of that black lace.)"

"The master-sculptor, Luca Lomi—an old family, once noble, but down in the world now. The master is obliged to make statues to get a living for his daughter and himself."

"More of the lace—double it over the bosom of the dress. And how is sitting to this needy sculptor to make your fortune?"

"Wait a minute. There are other sculptors besides him in the studio. There is, first, his brother, the priest—Father Rocco, who passes all his spare time with the master. He is a good sculptor in his way—has cast statues and made a font for his church—a holy man, who devotes all his work in the studio to the cause of piety."

"Ah, bah! we should think him a droll priest in France. (More pins.) You don't expect *him* to put money in your pocket, surely?"

"Wait, I say again. There is a third sculptor in the studio—actually a nobleman! His name is Fabio d'Ascoli. He is rich, young, handsome, an only child, and little better than a fool. Fancy his working at sculpture, as if he had his bread to get by it—and thinking that an amusement! Imagine a man belonging to one of the best families in Pisa mad enough to want to make a reputation as an artist! Wait! wait! the best is to come. His father and mother are dead—he has no near relations in the world to exercise authority over him—he is a bachelor, and his fortune is all at his own disposal; going a-begging, my friend; absolutely going a-begging for want of a clever woman to hold out her hand and take it from him."

"Yes, yes—now I understand. The goddess Minerva is a clever woman, and she will hold out her hand and take his fortune from him with the utmost docility."

"The first thing is to get him to offer it. I must tell you that I am not going to sit to him, but to his master, Luca Lomi, who is doing the statue of Minerva. The face is modeled from his daughter; and now he wants somebody to sit for the bust and arms. Maddalena Lomi and I are as nearly as possible the same height, I hear—the difference between us being that I have a good figure and she has a bad one. I have offered to sit, through a friend who is employed in the studio. If the master accepts, I am sure of an introduction to our rich young gentleman; and then leave it to my good looks, my various accomplishments, and my ready tongue, to do the rest."

"Stop! I won't have the lace doubled, on second thoughts. I'll have it single, and running all round the dress in curves—so. Well, and who is this friend of yours employed in the studio? A fourth sculptor?"

"No, no; the strangest, simplest little creature—"

Just then a faint tap was audible at the door of the room.

Brigida laid her finger on her lips, and called impatiently to the person outside to come in.

The door opened gently, and a young girl, poorly but very neatly dressed, entered the room. She was rather thin and under the average height; but her head and figure were in perfect proportion. Her hair was of that gorgeous auburn color, her eyes of that deep violet-blue, which the portraits of Giorgione and Titian have made famous as the type of Venetian beauty. Her features possessed the definiteness and regularity, the "good modeling" (to use an artist's term), which is the rarest of all womanly charms, in Italy as elsewhere. The one serious defect of her face was its paleness. Her cheeks, wanting nothing in form, wanted everything in color. That look of health, which is the essential crowning-point of beauty, was the one attraction which her face did not possess.

She came into the room with a sad and weary expression in her eyes, which changed, however, the moment she observed the magnificently-dressed French forewoman, into a look of astonishment, and almost of awe. Her manner became shy and embarrassed; and after an instant of hesitation, she turned back silently to the door.

"Stop, stop, Nanina," said Brigida, in Italian. "Don't be afraid of that lady. She is our new forewoman; and she has it in her power to do all sorts of kind things for you. Look up, and tell us what you want. You were sixteen last birthday, Nanina, and you behave like a baby of two years old!"

"I only came to know if there was any work for me to-day," said the girl, in a very sweet voice, that trembled a little as she tried to face the fashionable French forewoman again.

"No work, child, that is easy enough for you to do," said Brigida. "Are you going to the studio to-day?"

Some of the color that Nanina's cheeks wanted began to steal over them as she answered "Yes."

"Don't forget my message, darling. And if Master Luca Lomi asks where I live, answer that you are ready to deliver a letter to me; but that you are forbidden to enter into any particulars at first about who I am, or where I live."

"Why am I forbidden?" inquired Nanina, innocently.

"Don't ask questions, baby! Do as you are told. Bring me back a nice note or message to-morrow from the studio, and I will intercede with this lady to get you some work. You are a foolish child to want it, when you might make more money here and at Florence, by sitting to painters and sculptors; though what they can see to paint or model in you I never could understand."

"I like working at home better than going abroad to sit," said Nanina, looking very much abashed as she faltered out the answer, and escaping from the room with a terrified farewell obeisance, which was an eccentric compound of a start, a bow, and a courtesy.

"That awkward child would be pretty," said Mademoiselle Virginie, making rapid progress with the cutting-out of her dress, "if she knew how to give herself a complexion, and had a presentable gown on her back. Who is she?"

"The friend who is to get me into Master Luca Lomi's studio," replied Brigida, laughing. "Rather a curious ally for me to take up with, isn't she?"

"Where did you meet with her?"

"Here, to be sure; she hangs about this place for any plain work she can get to do, and takes it home to the oddest little room in a street near the Campo Santo. I had the curiosity to follow her one day, and knocked at her door soon after she had gone in, as if I was a visitor. She answered my knock in a great flurry and fright, as you may imagine. I made myself agreeable, affected immense interest in her affairs, and so got into her room. Such a place! A mere corner of it curtained off to make a bedroom. One chair, one stool, one saucepan on the fire. Before the hearth the most grotesquely hideous unshaven poodle-dog you ever saw; and on the stool a fair little girl plaiting dinner-mats. Such was the household—furniture and all included. 'Where is your father?' I asked. 'He ran away and left us years ago,' answers my awkward little friend who has just left the room, speaking in that simple way of hers, with all the composure in the world. 'And your mother?'—'Dead.' She went up to the little mat-plaiting girl as she gave that answer, and began playing with her long flaxen hair. 'Your sister, I suppose,' said I. 'What is her name?'—'They call me La Biondella,' says the child, looking up from her mat (La Biondella, Virginie, means The Fair). 'And why do you let that great, shaggy, ill-looking brute lie before your fireplace?' I asked. 'Oh!' cried the little mat-plaiter, 'that is our dear old dog, Scarammuccia. He takes care of the house when Nanina is not at home. He dances on his hind legs, and jumps through a hoop, and tumbles down dead when I cry Bang! Scarammuccia followed us home one night, years ago, and he has lived with us ever since. He goes out every day by himself, we can't tell where, and generally returns licking his chops, which makes us afraid that he is a thief; but nobody finds him out, because he is the cleverest dog that ever lived!' The child ran on in this way about the great beast by the fireplace, till I was obliged to stop her; while that simpleton Nanina stood by, laughing and encouraging her. I asked them a few more questions, which produced some strange answers. They did not seem to know of any relations of theirs in the world. The neighbors in the house had helped them, after their father ran away, until they were old enough to help themselves; and they did not seem to think there was anything in the least wretched or pitiable in their way of living. The last thing I heard, when I left them that day, was La Biondella crying 'Bang!'—then a bark, a thump on the floor, and a scream of laughter. If it was not for their dog, I should go and see them oftener. But the ill-conditioned beast has taken a dislike to me, and growls and shows his teeth whenever I come near him."

"The girl looked sickly when she came in here. Is she always like that?"

"No. She has altered within the last month. I suspect our interesting young nobleman has produced an impression. The oftener the girl has sat to him lately, the paler and more out of spirits she has become."

"Oh! she has sat to him, has she?"

"She is sitting to him now. He is doing a bust of some Pagan nymph or other, and prevailed on Nanina to let him copy from her head and face. According to her own account the little fool was frightened at first, and gave him all the trouble in the world before she would consent."

"And now she has consented, don't you think it likely she may turn out rather a dangerous rival? Men are such fools, and take such fancies into their heads—"

"Ridiculous! A thread-paper of a girl like that, who has no manner, no talk, no intelligence; who has nothing to recommend her but an awkward, babyish prettiness! Dangerous to me? No, no! If there is danger at all, I have to dread it from the sculptor's daughter. I don't mind confessing that I am anxious to see Maddalena Lomi. But as for Nanina, she will simply be of use to me. All I know already about the studio and the artists in it, I know through her. She will deliver my message, and procure me my introduction; and when we have got so far, I shall give her an old gown and a shake of the hand; and then, good-by to our little innocent!"

"Well, well, for your sake I hope you are the wiser of the two in this matter. For my part, I always distrust innocence. Wait one moment, and I shall have the body and sleeves of this dress ready for the needle-women. There, ring the bell, and order them up; for I have directions to give, and you must interpret for me."

While Brigida went to the bell, the energetic Frenchwoman began planning out the skirt of the new dress. She laughed as she measured off yard after yard of the silk.

"What are you laughing about?" asked Brigida, opening the door and ringing a hand-bell in the passage.

"I can't help fancying, dear, in spite of her innocent face and her artless ways, that your young friend is a hypocrite."

"And I am quite certain, love, that she is only a simpleton."

II

The studio of the master-sculptor, Luca Lomi, was composed of two large rooms unequally divided by a wooden partition, with an arched doorway cut in the middle of it.

While the milliners of the Grifoni establishment were industriously shaping dresses, the sculptors in Luca Lomi's workshop were, in their way, quite as hard at work shaping marble and clay. In the smaller of the two rooms the young nobleman (only addressed in the studio by his Christian name of Fabio) was busily engaged on his bust, with Nanina sitting before him as a model. His was not one of those traditional Italian faces from which subtlety and suspicion are always supposed to look out darkly on the world at large. Both countenance and expression proclaimed his character frankly and freely to all who saw him. Quick intelligence looked brightly from his eyes; and easy good humor laughed out pleasantly in the rather quaint curve of his lips. For the rest, his face expressed the defects as well as the merits of his character, showing that he wanted resolution and perseverance just as plainly as it showed also that he possessed amiability and intelligence.

At the end of the large room, nearest to the street door, Luca Lomi was standing by his life-size statue of Minerva; and was issuing directions, from time to time, to some of his workmen, who were roughly chiseling the drapery of another figure. At the opposite side of the room, nearest to the partition, his brother, Father Rocco, was taking a cast from a statuette of the Madonna; while Maddalena Lomi, the sculptor's daughter, released from sitting for Minerva's face, walked about the two rooms, and watched what was going on in them.

There was a strong family likeness of a certain kind between father, brother and daughter. All three were tall, handsome, dark-haired, and dark-eyed; nevertheless, they differed in expression, strikingly as they resembled one another in feature. Maddalena Lomi's face betrayed strong passions, but not an ungenerous nature. Her father, with the same indications of a violent temper, had some sinister lines about his mouth and forehead which suggested anything rather than an open disposition. Father Rocco's countenance, on the other hand, looked like the personification of absolute calmness and invincible moderation; and his manner, which, in a very firm way, was singularly quiet and deliberate, assisted in carrying out the impression produced by his face.

The daughter seemed as if she could fly into a passion at a moment's notice, and forgive also at a moment's notice. The father, appearing to be just as irritable, had something in his face which said, as plainly as if in words, "Anger me, and I never pardon." The priest looked as if he need never be called on either to ask forgiveness or to grant it, for the double reason that he could irritate nobody else, and that nobody else could irritate him.

"Rocco," said Luca, looking at the face of his Minerva, which was now finished, "this statue of mine will make a sensation."

"I am glad to hear it," rejoined the priest, dryly.

"It is a new thing in art," continued Luca, enthusiastically. "Other sculptors, with a classical subject like mine, limit themselves to the ideal classical face, and never think of aiming at individual character. Now I do precisely the reverse of that. I get my handsome daughter, Maddalena, to sit for Minerva, and I make an exact likeness of her. I may lose in ideal beauty, but I gain in individual character. People may accuse me of disregarding established rules; but my answer is, that I make my own rules. My daughter looks like a Minerva, and there she is exactly as she looks."

"It is certainly a wonderful likeness," said Father Rocco, approaching the statue.

"It the girl herself," cried the other. "Exactly her expression, and exactly her features. Measure Maddalena, and measure Minerva, and from forehead to chin, you won't find a hair-breadth of difference between them."

"But how about the bust and arms of the figure, now the face is done?" asked the priest, returning, as he spoke, to his own work.

"I may have the very model I want for them to-morrow. Little Nanina has just given me the strangest message. What do you think of a mysterious lady admirer who offers to sit for the bust and arms of my Minerva?"

"Are you going to accept the offer?" inquired the priest.

"I am going to receive her to-morrow; and if I really find that she is the same height as Maddalena, and has a bust and arms worth modeling, of course I shall accept her offer; for she will be the very sitter I have been looking after for weeks past. Who can she be? That's the mystery I want to find out. Which do you say, Rocco—an enthusiast or an adventuress?"

"I do not presume to say, for I have no means of knowing."

"Ah, there you are with your moderation again. Now, I do presume to assert that she must be either one or the other—or she would not have forbidden Nanina to say anything about her in answer to all my first natural inquiries. Where is Maddalena? I thought she was here a minute ago."

"She is in Fabio's room," answered Father Rocco, softly. "Shall I call her?"

"No, no!" returned Luca. He stopped, looked round at the workmen, who were chipping away mechanically at their bit of drapery; then advanced close to the priest, with a cunning smile, and continued in a whisper, "If Maddalena can only get from Fabio's room here to Fabio's palace over the way, on the Arno—come, come, Rocco! don't shake your head. If I brought her up to your church door one of these days, as Fabio d'Ascoli's betrothed, you would be glad enough to take the rest of the business off my hands, and make her Fabio d'Ascoli's wife. You are a very holy man, Rocco, but you know the difference between the clink of the money-bag and the clink of the chisel for all that!"

"I am sorry to find, Luca," returned the priest, coldly, "that you allow yourself to talk of the most delicate subjects in the coarsest way. This is one of the minor sins of the tongue which is growing on you. When we are alone in the studio, I will endeavor to lead you into speaking of the young man in the room there, and of your daughter, in terms more becoming to you, to me, and to them. Until that time, allow me to go on with my work."

Luca shrugged his shoulders, and went back to his statue. Father Rocco, who had been engaged during the last ten minutes in mixing wet plaster to the right consistency for taking a cast, suspended his occupation; and crossing the room to a corner next the partition, removed from it a cheval-glass which stood there. He lifted it away gently, while his brother's back was turned, carried it close to the table at which he had been at work, and then resumed his employment of mixing the plaster. Having at last prepared the composition for use, he laid it over the exposed half of the statuette with a neatness and dexterity which showed him to be a practiced hand at cast-taking. Just as he had covered the necessary extent of surface, Luca turned round from his statue.

"How are you getting on with the cast?" he asked. "Do you want any help?"

"None, brother, I thank you," answered the priest. "Pray do not disturb either yourself or your workmen on my account."

Luca turned again to the statue; and, at the same moment, Father Rocco softly moved the cheval-glass toward the open doorway between the two rooms, placing it at such an angle as to make it reflect the figures of the persons in the smaller studio. He did this with significant quickness and precision. It was evidently not the first time he had used the glass for purposes of secret observation.

Mechanically stirring the wet plaster round and round for the second casting, the priest looked into the glass, and saw, as in a picture, all that was going forward in the inner room. Maddalena Lomi was standing behind the young nobleman, watching the progress he made with his bust. Occasionally she took the modeling tool out of his hand, and showed him, with her sweetest smile, that she, too, as a sculptor's daughter, understood something of the sculptor's art; and now and then, in the pauses of the conversation, when her interest was especially intense in Fabio's work, she suffered her hand to drop absently on his shoulder, or stooped forward so close to him that her hair mingled for a moment with his. Moving the glass an inch or two, so as to bring Nanina well under his eye, Father Rocco found that he could trace each repetition of these little acts of familiarity by the immediate effect which they produced on the girl's face and manner. Whenever Maddalena so much as touched the young nobleman—no matter whether she did so by premeditation, or really by accident—Nanina's features contracted, her pale cheeks grew paler, she fidgeted on her chair, and her fingers nervously twisted and untwisted the loose ends of the ribbon fastened round her waist.

"Jealous," thought Father Rocco; "I suspected it weeks ago."

He turned away, and gave his whole attention for a few minutes to the mixing of the plaster. When he looked back again at the glass, he was just in time to witness a little accident which suddenly changed the relative positions of the three persons in the inner room.

He saw Maddalena take up a modeling tool which lay on a table near her, and begin to help Fabio in altering the arrangement of the hair in his bust. The young man watched what she was doing earnestly enough for a few moments; then his attention wandered away to Nanina. She looked at him reproachfully, and he answered by a sign which brought a smile to her face directly. Maddalena surprised her at the instant of the change; and, following the direction of her eyes, easily discovered at whom the smile was directed. She darted a glance of contempt at Nanina, threw down the modeling tool, and turned indignantly to the young sculptor, who was affecting to be hard at work again.

"Signor Fabio," she said, "the next time you forget what is due to your rank and yourself, warn me of it, if you please, beforehand, and I will take care to leave the room." While speaking the last words, she passed through the doorway. Father Rocco, bending abstractedly over his plaster mixture, heard her continue to herself in a whisper, as she went by him, "If I have any influence at all with my father, that impudent beggar-girl shall be forbidden the studio."

"Jealousy on the other side," thought the priest. "Something must be done at once, or this will end badly."

He looked again at the glass, and saw Fabio, after an instant of hesitation, beckon to Nanina to approach him. She left her seat, advanced half-way to his, then stopped. He stepped forward to meet her, and, taking her by the hand, whispered earnestly in her ear. When he had done, before dropping her hand, he touched her cheek with his lips, and then helped her on with the little white mantilla which covered her head and shoulders out-of-doors. The girl trembled violently, and drew the linen close to her face as Fabio walked into the larger studio, and, addressing Father Rocco, said:

"I am afraid I am more idle, or more stupid, than ever to-day. I can't get on with the bust at all to my satisfaction, so I have cut short the sitting, and given Nanina a half-holiday."

At the first sound of his voice, Maddalena, who was speaking to her father, stopped, and, with another look of scorn at Nanina standing trembling in the doorway, left the room. Luca Lomi called Fabio to him as she went away, and Father Rocco, turning to the statuette, looked to see how the plaster was hardening on it. Seeing them thus engaged, Nanina attempted to escape from the studio without being noticed; but the priest stopped her just as she was hurrying by him.

"My child," said he, in his gentle, quiet way, "are you going home?"

Nanina's heart beat too fast for her to reply in words; she could only answer by bowing her head.

"Take this for your little sister," pursued Father Rocco, putting a few silver coins in her hand; "I have got some customers for those mats she plaits so nicely. You need not bring them to my rooms; I will come and see you this evening, when I am going my rounds among my parishioners, and will take the mats away with me. You are a good girl, Nanina—you have always been a good girl—and as long as I am alive, my child, you shall never want a friend and an adviser."

Nanina's eyes filled with tears. She drew the mantilla closer than ever round her face, as she tried to thank the priest. Father Rocco nodded to her kindly, and laid his hand lightly on her head for a moment, then turned round again to his cast.

"Don't forget my message to the lady who is to sit to me to-morrow," said Luca to Nanina, as she passed him on her way out of the studio.

After she had gone, Fabio returned to the priest, who was still busy over his cast.

"I hope you will get on better with the bust to-morrow," said Father Rocco, politely; "I am sure you cannot complain of your model."

"Complain of her!" cried the young man, warmly; "she has the most beautiful head I ever saw. If I were twenty times the sculptor that I am, I should despair of being able to do her justice."

He walked into the inner room to look at his bust again—lingered before it for a little while—and then turned to retrace his steps to the larger studio. Between him and the doorway stood three chairs. As he went by them, he absently touched the backs of the first two, and passed the third; but just as he was entering the larger room, stopped, as if struck by a sudden recollection, returned hastily, and touched the third chair. Raising his eyes, as he approached the large studio again after doing this, he met the eyes of the priest fixed on him in unconcealed astonishment.

"Signor Fabio!" exclaimed Father Rocco, with a sarcastic smile, "who would ever have imagined that you were superstitious?"

"My nurse was," returned the young man, reddening, and laughing rather uneasily. "She taught me some bad habits that I have not got over yet." With those words he nodded and hastily went out.

"Superstitious," said Father Rocco softly to himself. He smiled again, reflected for a moment, and then, going to the window, looked into the street. The way to the left led to Fabio's palace, and the way to the right to the Campo Santo, in the neighborhood of which Nanina lived. The priest was just in time to see the young sculptor take the way to the right.

After another half-hour had elapsed, the two workmen quitted the studio to go to dinner, and Luca and his brother were left alone.

"We may return now," said Father Rocco, "to that conversation which was suspended between us earlier in the day."

"I have nothing more to say," rejoined Luca, sulkily.

"Then you can listen to me, brother, with the greater attention," pursued the priest. "I objected to the coarseness of your tone in talking of our young pupil and your daughter; I object still more strongly to your insinuation that my desire to see them married (provided always that they are sincerely attached to each other) springs from a mercenary motive."

"You are trying to snare me, Rocco, in a mesh of fine phrases; but I am not to be caught. I know what my own motive is for hoping that Maddalena may get an offer of marriage from this wealthy young gentleman—she will have his money, and we shall all profit by it. That is coarse and mercenary, if you please; but it is the true reason why I want to see Maddalena married to Fabio. You want to see it, too—and for what reason, I should like to know, if not for mine?"

"Of what use would wealthy relations be to me? What are people with money—what is money itself—to a man who follows my calling?"

"Money is something to everybody."

"Is it? When have you found that I have taken any account of it? Give me money enough to buy my daily bread, and to pay for my lodging and my coarse cassock, and though I may want much for the poor, for myself I want no more. Then have you found me mercenary? Do I not help you in this studio, for love of you and of the art, without exacting so much as journeyman's wages? Have I ever asked you for more than a few crowns to give away on feast-days among my parishioners? Money! money for a man who may be summoned to Rome to-morrow, who may be told to go at half an hour's notice on a foreign mission that may take him to the ends of the earth, and who would be ready to go the moment when he was called on! Money to a man who has no wife, no children, no interests outside the sacred circle of the Church! Brother, do you see the dust and dirt and shapeless marble chips lying around your statue there? Cover that floor instead with gold, and, though the litter may have changed in color and form, in my eyes it would be litter still."

"A very noble sentiment, I dare say, Rocco, but I can't echo it. Granting that you care nothing for money, will you explain to me why you are so anxious that Maddalena should marry Fabio? She has had offers from poorer men—you knew of them—but you have never taken the least interest in her accepting or rejecting a proposal before."

"I hinted the reason to you, months ago, when Fabio first entered the studio."

"It was rather a vague hint, brother; can't you be plainer to-day?"

"I think I can. In the first place, let me begin by assuring you that I have no objection to the young man himself. He may be a little capricious and undecided, but he has no incorrigible faults that I have discovered."

"That is rather a cool way of praising him, Rocco."

"I should speak of him warmly enough, if he were not the representative of an intolerable corruption, and a monstrous wrong. Whenever I think of him I think of an injury which his present existence perpetuates; and if I do speak of him coldly, it is only for that reason."

Luca looked away quickly from his brother, and began kicking absently at the marble chips which were scattered over the floor around him.

"I now remember," he said, "what that hint of yours pointed at. I know what you mean."

"Then you know," answered the priest, "that while part of the wealth which Fabio d'Ascoli possesses is honestly and incontestably his own; part, also, has been inherited by him from the spoilers and robbers of the Church—"

"Blame his ancestors for that; don't blame him."

"I blame him as long as the spoil is not restored."

"How do you know that it was spoil, after all?"

"I have examined more carefully than most men the records of the civil wars in Italy; and I know that the ancestors of Fabio d'Ascoli wrung from the Church, in her hour of weakness, property which they dared to claim as their right. I know of titles to lands signed away, in those stormy times, under the influence of fear, or through false representations of which the law takes no account. I call the money thus obtained spoil, and I say that it ought to be restored, and shall be restored, to the Church from which it was taken."

"And what does Fabio answer to that, brother?"

"I have not spoken to him on the subject."

"Why not?"

"Because I have, as yet, no influence over him. When he is married, his wife will have influence over him, and she shall speak."

"Maddalena, I suppose? How do you know that she will speak?"

"Have I not educated her? Does she not understand what her duties are toward the Church, in whose bosom she has been reared?"

Luca hesitated uneasily, and walked away a step or two before he spoke again.

"Does this spoil, as you call it, amount to a large sum of money?" he asked, in an anxious whisper.

"I may answer that question, Luca, at some future time," said the priest. "For the present, let it be enough that you are acquainted with all I undertook to inform you of when we began our conversation. You now know that if I am anxious for this marriage to take place, it is from motives entirely unconnected with self-interest. If all the property which Fabio's ancestors wrongfully obtained from the Church were restored to the Church to-morrow, not one paulo of it would go into my pocket. I am a poor priest now, and to the end of my days shall remain so. You soldiers of the world, brother, fight for your pay; I am a soldier of the Church, and I fight for my cause."

Saying these words, he returned abruptly to the statuette; and refused to speak, or leave his employment again, until he had taken the mold off, and had carefully put away the various fragments of which it consisted. This done, he drew a writing-desk from the drawer of his working-table, and taking out a slip of paper wrote these lines:

"Come down to the studio to-morrow. Fabio will be with us, but Nanina will return no more."

Without signing what he had written, he sealed it up, and directed it to "Donna Maddalena"; then took his hat, and handed the note to his brother.

"Oblige me by giving that to my niece," he said.

"Tell me, Rocco," said Luca, turning the note round and round perplexedly between his finger and thumb; "do you think Maddalena will be lucky enough to get married to Fabio?"

"Still coarse in your expressions, brother!"

"Never mind my expressions. Is it likely?"

"Yes, Luca, I think it is likely."

With those words he waved his hand pleasantly to his brother, and went out.

III

From the studio Father Rocco went straight to his own rooms, hard by the church to which he was attached. Opening a cabinet in his study, he took from one of its drawers a handful of small silver money, consulted for a minute or so a slate on which several names and addresses were written, provided himself with a portable inkhorn and some strips of paper, and again went out.

He directed his steps to the poorest part of the neighborhood; and entering some very wretched houses, was greeted by the inhabitants with great respect and affection. The women, especially, kissed his hands with more reverence than they would have shown to the highest crowned head in Europe. In return, he talked to them as easily and unconstrainedly as if they were his equals; sat down cheerfully on dirty bedsides and rickety benches; and distributed his little gifts of money with the air of a man who was paying debts rather than bestowing charity. Where he encountered cases of illness, he pulled out his inkhorn and slips of paper, and wrote simple prescriptions to be made up from the medicine-chest of a neighboring convent, which served the same merciful purpose then that is answered by dispensaries in our days. When he had exhausted his money, and had got through his visits, he was escorted out of the poor quarter by a perfect train of enthusiastic followers. The women kissed his hand again, and the men uncovered as he turned, and, with a friendly sign, bade them all farewell.

As soon as he was alone again, he walked toward the Campo Santo, and, passing the house in which Nanina lived, sauntered up and down the street thoughtfully for some minutes. When he at length ascended the steep staircase that led to the room occupied by the sisters, he found the door ajar. Pushing it open gently, he saw La Biondella sitting with her pretty, fair profile turned toward him, eating her evening meal of bread and grapes. At the opposite end of the room, Scarammuccia was perched up on his hindquarters in a corner, with his mouth wide open to catch the morsel of bread which he evidently expected the child to throw to him. What the elder sister was doing, the priest had not time to see; for the dog barked the moment he presented himself, and Nanina hastened to the door to ascertain who the intruder might be. All that he could observe was that she was too confused, on catching sight of him, to be able to utter a word. La Biondella was the first to speak.

"Thank you, Father Rocco," said the child, jumping up, with her bread in one hand and her grapes in the other—"thank you for giving me so much money for my dinner-mats. There they are, tied up together in one little parcel, in the corner. Nanina said she was ashamed to think of your carrying them; and I said I knew where you lived, and I should like to ask you to let me take them home!"

"Do you think you can carry them all the way, my dear?" asked the priest.

"Look, Father Rocco, see if I can't carry them!" cried La Biondella, cramming her bread into one of the pockets of her little apron, holding her bunch of grapes by the stalk in her mouth, and hoisting the packet of dinner-mats on her head in a moment. "See, I am strong enough to carry double," said the child, looking up proudly into the priest's face.

"Can you trust her to take them home for me?" asked Father Rocco, turning to Nanina. "I want to speak to you alone, and her absence will give me the opportunity. Can you trust her out by herself?"

"Yes, Father Rocco, she often goes out alone." Nanina gave this answer in low, trembling tones, and looked down confusedly on the ground.

"Go then, my dear," said Father Rocco, patting the child on the shoulder; "and come back here to your sister, as soon as you have left the mats."

La Biondella went out directly in great triumph, with Scarammuccia walking by her side, and keeping his muzzle suspiciously close to the pocket in which she had put her bread. Father Rocco closed the door after them, and then, taking the one chair which the room possessed, motioned to Nanina to sit by him on the stool.

"Do you believe that I am your friend, my child, and that I have always meant well toward you?" he began.

"The best and kindest of friends," answered Nanina.

"Then you will hear what I have to say patiently, and you will believe that I am speaking for your good, even if my words should distress you?" (Nanina turned away her head.) "Now, tell me; should I be wrong, to begin with, if I said that my brother's pupil, the young nobleman whom we call 'Signor Fabio,' had been here to see you to-day?" (Nanina started up affrightedly from her stool.) "Sit down again, my child; I am not going to blame you. I am only going to tell you what you must do for the future."

He took her hand; it was cold, and it trembled violently in his.

"I will not ask what he has been saying to you," continued the priest; "for it might distress you to answer, and I have, moreover, had means of knowing that your youth and beauty have made a strong impression on him. I will pass over, then, all reference to the words he may have been speaking to you; and I will come at once to what I have now to say, in my turn. Nanina, my child, arm yourself with all your courage, and promise me, before we part to-night, that you will see Signor Fabio no more."

Nanina turned round suddenly, and fixed her eyes on him, with an expression of terrified incredulity. "No more?"

"You are very young and very innocent," said Father Rocco; "but surely you must have thought before now of the difference between Signor Fabio and you. Surely you must have often remembered that you are low down among the ranks of the poor, and that he is high up among the rich and the nobly born?"

Nanina's hands dropped on the priest's knees. She bent her head down on them, and began to weep bitterly.

"Surely you must have thought of that?" reiterated Father Rocco.

"Oh, I have often, often thought of it!" murmured the girl "I have mourned over it, and cried about it in secret for many nights past. He said I looked pale, and ill, and out of spirits to-day, and I told him it was with thinking of that!"

"And what did he say in return?"

There was no answer. Father Rocco looked down. Nanina raised her head directly from his knees, and tried to turn it away again. He took her hand and stopped her.

"Come!" he said; "speak frankly to me. Say what you ought to say to your father and your friend. What was his answer, my child, when you reminded him of the difference between you?"

"He said I was born to be a lady," faltered the girl, still struggling to turn her face away, "and that I might make myself one if I would learn and be patient. He said that if he had all the noble ladies in Pisa to choose from on one side, and only little Nanina on the other, he would hold out his hand to me, and tell them, 'This shall be my wife.' He said love knew no difference of rank; and that if he was a nobleman and rich, it was all the more reason why he should please himself. He was so kind, that I thought my heart would burst while he was speaking; and my little sister liked him so, that she got upon his knee and kissed him. Even our dog, who growls at other strangers, stole to his side and licked his hand. Oh, Father Rocco! Father Rocco!" The tears burst out afresh, and the lovely head dropped once more, wearily, on the priest's knee.

Father Rocco smiled to himself, and waited to speak again till she was calmer.

"Supposing," he resumed, after some minutes of silence, "supposing Signor Fabio really meant all he said to you—"

Nanina started up, and confronted the priest boldly for the first time since he had entered the room.

"Supposing!" she exclaimed, her cheeks beginning to redden, and her dark blue eyes flashing suddenly through her tears "Supposing! Father Rocco, Fabio would never deceive me. I would die here at your feet, rather than doubt the least word he said to me!"

The priest signed to her quietly to return to the stool. "I never suspected the child had so much spirit in her," he thought to himself.

"I would die," repeated Nanina, in a voice that began to falter now. "I would die rather than doubt him."

"I will not ask you to doubt him," said Father Rocco, gently; "and I will believe in him myself as firmly as you do. Let us suppose, my child, that you have learned patiently all the many things of which you are now ignorant, and which it is necessary for a lady to know. Let us suppose that Signor Fabio has really violated all the laws that govern people in his high station and has taken you to him publicly as his wife. You would be happy then, Nanina; but would he? He has no father or mother to control him, it is true; but he has friends—many friends and intimates in his own rank—proud, heartless people, who know nothing of your worth and goodness; who, hearing of your low birth, would look on you, and on your husband too, my child, with contempt. He has not your patience and fortitude. Think how bitter it would be for him to bear that contempt—to see you shunned by proud women, and carelessly pitied or patronized by insolent men. Yet all this, and more, he would have to endure, or else to quit the world he has lived in from his boyhood—the world he was born to live in. You love him, I know—"

Nanina's tears burst out afresh. "Oh, how dearly—how dearly!" she murmured.

"Yes, you love him dearly," continued the priest; "but would all your love compensate him for everything else that he must lose? It might, at first; but there would come a time when the world would assert its influence over him again; when he would feel a want which you could not supply—a weariness which you could not solace. Think of his life then, and of yours. Think of the first day when the first secret doubt whether he had done rightly in marrying you would steal into his mind. We are not masters of all our impulses. The lightest spirits have their moments of irresistible depression; the bravest hearts are not always superior to doubt. My child, my child, the world is strong, the pride of rank is rooted deep, and the human will is frail at best! Be warned! For your own sake and for Fabio's, be warned in time."

Nanina stretched out her hands toward the priest in despair.

"Oh, Father Rocco! Father Rocco!" she cried, "why did you not tell me this before?"

"Because, my child, I only knew of the necessity for telling you to-day. But it is not too late; it is never too late to do a good action. You love Fabio, Nanina? Will you prove that love by making a great sacrifice for his good?"

"I would die for his good!"

"Will you nobly cure him of a passion which will be his ruin, if not yours, by leaving Pisa to-morrow?"

"Leave Pisa!" exclaimed Nanina. Her face grew deadly pale; she rose and moved back a step or two from the priest.

"Listen to me," pursued Father Rocco; "I have heard you complain that you could not get regular employment at needle-work. You shall have that employment, if you will go with me—you and your little sister too, of course—to Florence to-morrow."

"I promised Fabio to go to the studio," began Nanina, affrightedly. "I promised to go at ten o'clock. How can I—"

She stopped suddenly, as if her breath were failing her.

"I myself will take you and your sister to Florence," said Father Rocco, without noticing the interruption. "I will place you under the care of a lady who will be as kind as a mother to you both. I will answer for your getting such work to do as will enable you to keep yourself honestly and independently; and I will undertake, if you do not like your life at Florence, to bring you back to Pisa after a lapse of three months only. Three months, Nanina. It is not a long exile."

"Fabio! Fabio!" cried the girl, sinking again on the seat, and hiding her face.

"It is for his good," said Father Rocco, calmly: "for Fabio's good, remember."

"What would he think of me if I went away? Oh, if I had but learned to write! If I could only write Fabio a letter!"

"Am I not to be depended on to explain to him all that he ought to know?"

"How can I go away from him! Oh! Father Rocco, how can you ask me to go away from him?"

"I will ask you to do nothing hastily. I will leave you till to-morrow morning to decide. At nine o'clock I shall be in the street; and I will not even so much as enter this house, unless I know beforehand that you have resolved to follow my advice. Give me a sign from your window. If I see you wave your white mantilla out of it, I shall know that you have taken the noble resolution to save Fabio and to save yourself. I will say no more, my child; for, unless I am grievously mistaken in you, I have already said enough."

He went out, leaving her still weeping bitterly. Not far from the house, he met La Biondella and the dog on their way back. The little girl stopped to report to him the safe delivery of her dinner-mats; but he passed on quickly with a nod and a smile. His interview with Nanina had left some influence behind it, which unfitted him just then for the occupation of talking to a child.

NEARLY HALF AN HOUR BEFORE nine o'clock on the following morning, Father Rocco set forth for the street in which Nanina lived. On his way thither he overtook a dog walking lazily a few paces ahead in the roadway; and saw, at the same time, an elegantly-dressed lady advancing toward him. The dog stopped suspiciously as she approached, and growled and showed his teeth when she passed him. The lady, on her side, uttered an exclamation of disgust, but did not seem to be either astonished or frightened by the animal's threatening attitude. Father Rocco looked after her with some curiosity as she walked by him. She was a handsome woman, and he admired her courage. "I know that growling brute well enough," he said to himself, "but who can the lady be?"

The dog was Scarammuccia, returning from one of his marauding expeditions The lady was Brigida, on her way to Luca Lomi's studio.

Some minutes before nine o'clock the priest took his post in the street, opposite Nanina's window. It was open; but neither she nor her little sister appeared at it. He looked up anxiously as the church-clocks struck the hour; but there was no sign for a minute or so after they were all silent. "Is she hesitating still?" said Father Rocco to himself.

Just as the words passed his lips, the white mantilla was waved out of the window.

WILKIE COLLINS

PART SECOND

I

Even the master-stroke of replacing the treacherous Italian forewoman by a French dressmaker, engaged direct from Paris, did not at first avail to elevate the great Grifoni establishment above the reach of minor calamities. Mademoiselle Virginie had not occupied her new situation at Pisa quite a week before she fell ill. All sorts of reports were circulated as to the cause of this illness; and the Demoiselle Grifoni even went so far as to suggest that the health of the new forewoman had fallen a sacrifice to some nefarious practices of the chemical sort, on the part of her rival in the trade. But, however the misfortune had been produced, it was a fact that Mademoiselle Virginie was certainly very ill, and another fact that the doctor insisted on her being sent to the baths of Lucca as soon as she could be moved from her bed.

Fortunately for the Demoiselle Grifoni, the Frenchwoman had succeeded in producing three specimens of her art before her health broke down. They comprised the evening-dress of yellow brocaded silk, to which she had devoted herself on the morning when she first assumed her duties at Pisa; a black cloak and hood of an entirely new shape; and an irresistibly fascinating dressing-gown, said to have been first brought into fashion by the princesses of the blood-royal of France. These articles of costume, on being exhibited in the showroom, electrified the ladies of Pisa; and orders from all sides flowed in immediately on the Grifoni establishment. They were, of course, easily executed by the inferior work-women, from the specimen designs of the French dressmaker. So that the illness of Mademoiselle Virginie, though it might cause her mistress some temporary inconvenience, was, after all, productive of no absolute loss.

Two months at the baths of Lucca restored the new forewoman to health. She returned to Pisa, and resumed her place in the private work-room. Once re-established there, she discovered that an important change had taken place during her absence. Her friend and assistant, Brigida, had resigned her situation. All inquiries made of the Demoiselle Grifoni only elicited one answer: the missing work-woman had abruptly left her place at five minutes' warning, and had departed without confiding to any one what she thought of doing, or whither she intended to turn her steps.

Months elapsed The new year came; but no explanatory letter arrived from Brigida. The spring season passed off, with all its accompaniments of dressmaking and dress-buying, but still there was no news of her. The first anniversary of Mademoiselle Virginie's engagement with the Demoiselle Grifoni came round; and then at last a note arrived, stating that Brigida had returned to Pisa, and that if the French forewoman would send an answer, mentioning where her private lodgings were, she would visit her old friend that evening after business hours. The information was gladly enough given; and, punctually to the appointed time, Brigida arrived in Mademoiselle Virginie's little sitting-room.

Advancing with her usual indolent stateliness of gait, the Italian asked after her friend's health as coolly, and sat down in the nearest chair as carelessly, as if they had not been separated for more than a few days. Mademoiselle Virginie laughed in her liveliest manner, and raised her mobile French eyebrows in sprightly astonishment.

"Well, Brigida!" she exclaimed, "they certainly did you no injustice when they nicknamed you 'Care-for-Nothing,' in old Grifoni's workroom. Where have you been? Why have you never written to me?"

"I had nothing particular to write about; and besides, I always intended to come back to Pisa and see you," answered Brigida, leaning back luxuriously in her chair.

"But where have you been for nearly a whole year past? In Italy?"

"No; at Paris. You know I can sing—not very well; but I have a voice, and most Frenchwomen (excuse the impertinence) have none. I met with a friend, and got introduced to a manager; and I have been singing at the theater—not the great parts, only the second. Your amiable countrywomen could not screech me down on the stage, but they intrigued against me successfully behind the scenes. In short, I quarreled with our principal lady, quarreled with the manager, quarreled with my friend; and here I am back at Pisa, with a little money saved in my pocket, and no great notion what I am to do next."

"Back at Pisa? Why did you leave it?"

Brigida's eyes began to lose their indolent expression. She sat up suddenly in her chair, and set one of her hands heavily on a little table by her side.

"Why?" she repeated. "Because when I find the game going against me, I prefer giving it up at once to waiting to be beaten."

"Ah! you refer to that last year's project of yours for making your fortune among the sculptors. I should like to hear how it was you failed with the wealthy young amateur. Remember that I fell ill before you had any news to give me. Your absence when I returned from Lucca, and, almost immediately afterward, the marriage of your intended conquest to the sculptor's daughter, proved to me, of course, that you must have failed. But I never heard how. I know nothing at this moment but the bare fact that Maddalena Lomi won the prize."

"Tell me first, do she and her husband live together happily?"

"There are no stories of their disagreeing. She has dresses, horses, carriages; a negro page, the smallest lap-dog in Italy—in short, all the luxuries that a woman can want; and a child, by-the-by, into the bargain."

"A child?"

"Yes; a child, born little more than a week ago."

"Not a boy, I hope?"

"No; a girl."

"I am glad of that. Those rich people always want the first-born to be an heir. They will both be disappointed. I am glad of that."

"Mercy on us, Brigida, how fierce you look!"

"Do I? It's likely enough. I hate Fabio d'Ascoli and Maddalena Lomi—singly as man and woman, doubly as man and wife. Stop! I'll tell you what you want to know directly. Only answer me another question or two first. Have you heard anything about her health?"

"How should I hear? Dressmakers can't inquire at the doors of the nobility."

"True. Now one last question. That little simpleton, Nanina?"

"I have never seen or heard anything of her. She can't be at Pisa, or she would have called at our place for work."

"Ah! I need not have asked about her if I had thought a moment beforehand. Father Rocco would be sure to keep her out of Fabio's sight, for his niece's sake."

"What, he really loved that 'thread-paper of a girl' as you called her?"

"Better than fifty such wives as he has got now! I was in the studio the morning he was told of her departure from Pisa. A letter was privately given to him, telling him that the girl had left the place out of a feeling of honor, and had hidden herself beyond the possibility of discovery, to prevent him from compromising himself with all his friends by marrying her. Naturally enough, he would not believe that this was her own doing; and, naturally enough also, when Father Rocco was sent for, and was not to be found, he suspected the priest of being at the bottom of the business. I never saw a man in such a fury of despair and rage before. He swore that he would have all Italy searched for the girl, that he would be the death of the priest, and that he would never enter Luca Lomi's studio again—"

"And, as to this last particular, of course, being a man, he failed to keep his word?"

"Of course. At that first visit of mine to the studio I discovered two things. The first, as I said, that Fabio was really in love with the girl—the second, that Maddalena Lomi was really in love with him. You may suppose I looked at her attentively while the disturbance was going on, and while nobody's notice was directed on me. All women are vain, I know, but vanity never blinded my eyes. I saw directly that I had but one superiority over her—my figure. She was my height, but not well made. She had hair as dark and as glossy as mine; eyes as bright and as black as mine; and the rest of her face better than mine. My nose is coarse, my lips are too thick, and my upper lip overhangs my under too far. She had none of those personal faults; and, as for capacity, she managed the young fool in his passion as well as I could have managed him in her place."

"How?"

"She stood silent, with downcast eyes and a distressed look, all the time he was raving up and down the studio. She must have hated the girl, and been rejoiced at her disappearance; but she never showed it. 'You would be an awkward rival' (I thought to myself), 'even to a handsomer woman than I am.' However, I determined not to despair too soon, and made up my mind to follow my plan just as if the accident of the girl's disappearance had never occurred. I smoothed down the master-sculptor easily enough—flattering him about his reputation, assuring him that the works of Luca Lomi had been the objects of my adoration since childhood, telling him that I had heard of his difficulty in finding a model to complete his Minerva from, and offering myself (if he thought me worthy) for the honor—laying great stress on that word—for the honor of sitting to him. I don't know whether he was altogether deceived by what I told him; but he was sharp enough to see that I really could be of use, and he accepted my offer with a profusion of compliments. We parted, having arranged that I was to give him a first sitting in a week's time."

"Why put it off so long?"

"To allow our young gentleman time to cool down and return to the studio, to be sure. What was the use of my being there while he was away?"

"Yes, yes—I forgot. And how long was it before he came back?"

"I had allowed him more time than enough. When I had given my first sitting I saw him in the studio, and heard it was his second visit there since the day of the girl's disappearance. Those very violent men are always changeable and irresolute."

"Had he made no attempt, then, to discover Nanina?"

"Oh, yes! He had searched for her himself, and had set others searching for her, but to no purpose. Four days of perpetual disappointment had been enough to bring him to his senses. Luca Lomi had written him a peace-making letter, asking what harm he or his daughter had done, even supposing Father Rocco was to blame. Maddalena Lomi had met him in the street, and had looked resignedly away from him, as if she expected him to pass her. In short, they had awakened his sense of justice and his good nature (you see, I can impartially give him his due), and they had got him back. He was silent and sentimental enough at first, and shockingly sulky and savage with the priest—"

"I wonder Father Rocco ventured within his reach."

"Father Rocco is not a man to be daunted or defeated by anybody, I can tell you. The same day on which Fabio came back to the studio, he returned to it. Beyond boldly declaring that he thought Nanina had done quite right, and had acted like a good and virtuous girl, he would say nothing about her or her disappearance. It was quite useless to ask him questions—he denied that any one had a right to put them. Threatening, entreating, flattering—all modes of appeal were thrown away on him. Ah, my dear! depend upon it, the cleverest and politest man in Pisa, the most dangerous to an enemy and the most delightful to a friend, is Father Rocco. The rest of them, when I began to play my cards a little too openly, behaved with brutal rudeness to me. Father Rocco, from first to last, treated me like a lady. Sincere or not, I don't care—he treated me like a lady when the others treated me like—"

"There! there! don't get hot about it now. Tell me instead how you made your first approaches to the young gentleman whom you talk of so contemptuously as Fabio."

"As it turned out, in the worst possible way. First, of course, I made sure of interesting him in me by telling him that I had known Nanina. So far it was all well enough. My next object was to persuade him that she could never have gone away if she had truly loved him alone; and that he must have had some fortunate rival in her own rank of life, to whom she had sacrificed him, after gratifying her vanity for a time by bringing a young nobleman to her feet. I had, as you will easily imagine, difficulty enough in making him take this view of Nanina's flight. His pride and his love for the girl were both concerned in refusing to admit the truth of my suggestion. At last I succeeded. I brought him to that state of ruffled vanity and fretful self-assertion in which it is easiest to work on a man's feelings—in which a man's own wounded pride makes the best pitfall to catch him in. I brought him, I say, to that state, and then *she* stepped in and profited by what I had done. Is it wonderful now that I rejoice in her disappointments—that I should be glad to hear any ill thing of her that any one could tell me?"

"But how did she first get the advantage of you?"

"If I had found out, she would never have succeeded where I failed. All I know is, that she had more opportunities of seeing him than I, and that she used them cunningly enough even to deceive me. While I thought I was gaining ground with Fabio, I was actually losing it. My first suspicions were excited by a change in Luca Lomi's conduct toward me. He grew cold, neglectful—at last absolutely rude. I was resolved not to see this; but accident soon obliged me to open my eyes. One morning I heard Fabio and Maddalena talking of me when they imagined I had left the studio. I can't repeat their words, especially here. The blood flies into my head, and the cold catches me at the heart, when I only think of them. It will be enough if I tell you that he laughed at me, and that she—"

"Hush! not so loud. There are other people lodging in the house. Never mind about telling me what you heard; it only irritates you to no purpose. I can guess that they had discovered—"

"Through her—remember, all through her!"

"Yes, yes, I understand. They had discovered a great deal more than you ever intended them to know, and all through her."

"But for the priest, Virginie, I should have been openly insulted and driven from their doors. He had insisted on their behaving with decent civility toward me. They said that he was afraid of me, and laughed at the notion of his trying to make them afraid too. That was the last thing I heard. The fury I was in, and the necessity of keeping it down, almost suffocated me. I turned round to leave the place forever, when, who should I see, standing close behind me, but Father Rocco. He must have discovered in my face that I knew all, but he took no notice of it. He only asked, in his usual quiet, polite way, if I was looking for anything I had lost, and if he could help me. I managed to thank him, and to get to the door. He opened it for me respectfully, and bowed—he treated me like a lady to the last! It was evening when I left the studio in that way. The next morning I threw up my situation, and turned my back on Pisa. Now you know everything."

"Did you hear of the marriage? or did you only assume from what you knew that it would take place?"

"I heard of it about six months ago. A man came to sing in the chorus at our theater who had been employed some time before at the grand concert given on the occasion of the marriage. But let us drop the subject now. I am in a fever already with talking of it. You are in a bad situation here, my dear; I declare your room is almost stifling."

"Shall I open the other window?"

"No; let us go out and get a breath of air by the river-side. Come! take your hood and fan—it is getting dark—nobody will see us, and we can come back here, if you like, in half an hour."

Mademoiselle Virginie acceded to her friend's wish rather reluctantly. They walked toward the river. The sun was down, and the sudden night of Italy was gathering fast. Although Brigida did not say another word on the subject of Fabio or his wife, she led the way to the bank of the Arno, on which the young nobleman's palace stood.

Just as they got near the great door of entrance, a sedan-chair, approaching in the opposite direction, was set down before it; and a footman, after a moment's conference with a lady inside the chair, advanced to the porter's lodge in the courtyard. Leaving her friend to go on, Brigida slipped in after the servant by the open wicket, and concealed herself in the shadow cast by the great closed gates.

"The Marchesa Melani, to inquire how the Countess d'Ascoli and the infant are this evening," said the footman.

"My mistress has not changed at all for the better since the morning," answered the porter. "The child is doing quite well."

The footman went back to the sedan-chair; then returned to the porter's lodge.

"The marchesa desires me to ask if fresh medical advice has been sent for," he said.

"Another doctor has arrived from Florence to-day," replied the porter.

Mademoiselle Virginie, missing her friend suddenly, turned back toward the palace to look after her, and was rather surprised to see Brigida slip out of the wicket-gate. There were two oil lamps burning on pillars outside the doorway, and their light glancing on the Italian's face, as she passed under them, showed that she was smiling.

II

While the Marchesa Melani was making inquiries at the gate of the palace, Fabio was sitting alone in the apartment which his wife usually occupied when she was in health. It was her favorite room, and had been prettily decorated, by her own desire, with hangings in yellow satin and furniture of the same color. Fabio was now waiting in it, to hear the report of the doctors after their evening visit.

Although Maddalena Lomi had not been his first love, and although he had married her under circumstances which are generally and rightly considered to afford few chances of lasting happiness in wedded life, still they had lived together through the one year of their union tranquilly, if not fondly. She had molded herself wisely to his peculiar humors, had made the most of his easy disposition; and, when her quick temper had got the better of her, had seldom hesitated in her cooler moments to acknowledge that she had been wrong. She had been extravagant, it is true, and had irritated him by fits of unreasonable jealousy; but these were faults not to be thought of now. He could only remember that she was the mother of his child, and that she lay ill but two rooms away from him—dangerously ill, as the doctors had unwillingly confessed on that very day.

The darkness was closing in upon him, and he took up the handbell to ring for lights. When the servant entered there was genuine sorrow in his face, genuine anxiety in his voice, as he inquired for news from the sick-room. The man only answered that his mistress was still asleep, and then withdrew, after first leaving a sealed letter on the table by his master's side. Fabio summoned him back into the room, and asked when the letter had arrived. He replied that it had been delivered at the palace two days since, and that he had observed it lying unopened on a desk in his master's study.

Left alone again, Fabio remembered that the letter had arrived at a time when the first dangerous symptoms of his wife's illness had declared themselves, and that he had thrown it aside, after observing the address to be in a handwriting unknown to him. In his present state of suspense, any occupation was better than sitting idle. So he took up the letter with a sigh, broke the seal, and turned inquiringly to the name signed at the end.

It was "Nanina."

He started, and changed color. "A letter from her," he whispered to himself. "Why does it come at such a time as this?"

His face grew paler, and the letter trembled in his fingers. Those superstitious feelings which he had ascribed to the nursery influences of his childhood, when Father Rocco charged him with them in the studio, seemed to be overcoming him now. He hesitated, and listened anxiously in the direction of his wife's room, before reading the letter. Was its arrival ominous of good or evil? That was the thought in his heart as he drew the lamp near to him, and looked at the first lines.

"Am I wrong in writing to you?" (the letter began abruptly). "If I am, you have but to throw this little leaf of paper into the fire, and to think no more of it after it is burned up and gone. I can never reproach you for treating my letter in that way; for we are never likely to meet again.

"Why did I go away? Only to save you from the consequences of marrying a poor girl who was not fit to become your wife. It almost broke my heart to leave you; for I had nothing to keep up my courage but the remembrance that I was going away for your sake. I had to think of that, morning and night—to think of it always, or I am afraid I should have faltered in my resolution, and have gone back to Pisa. I longed so much at first to see you once more, only to tell you that Nanina was not heartless and ungrateful, and that you might pity her and think kindly of her, though you might love her no longer.

"Only to tell you that! If I had been a lady I might have told it to you in a letter; but I had never learned to write, and I could not prevail on myself to get others to take the pen for me. All I could do was to learn secretly how to write with my own hand. It was long, long work; but the uppermost thought in my heart was always the thought of justifying myself to you, and that made me patient and persevering. I learned, at last, to write so as not to be ashamed of myself, or to make you ashamed of me. I began a letter—my first letter to you—but I heard of your marriage before it was done, and then I had to tear the paper up, and put the pen down again.

"I had no right to come between you and your wife, even with so little a thing as a letter; I had no right to do anything but hope and pray for your happiness. Are you happy? I am sure you ought to be; for how can your wife help loving you?

"It is very hard for me to explain why I have ventured on writing now, and yet I can't think that I am doing wrong. I heard a few days ago (for I have a friend at Pisa who keeps me informed, by my own desire, of all the pleasant changes in your life)—I heard of your child being born; and I thought myself, after that, justified at last in writing to you. No letter from me, at such a time as this, can rob your child's mother of so much as a thought of yours that is due to her. Thus, at least, it seems to me. I wish so well to your child, that I cannot surely be doing wrong in writing these lines.

"I have said already what I wanted to say—what I have been longing to say for a whole year past. I have told you why I left Pisa; and have, perhaps, persuaded you that I have gone through some suffering, and borne some heart-aches for your sake. Have I more to write? Only a word or two, to tell you that I am earning my bread, as I always wished to earn it, quietly at home—at least, at what I must call home now. I am living with reputable people, and I want for nothing. La Biondella has grown very much; she would hardly be obliged to get on your knee to kiss you now; and she can plait her dinner-mats faster and more neatly than ever. Our old dog is with us, and has learned two new tricks; but you can't be expected to remember him, although you were the only stranger I ever saw him take kindly to at first.

"It is time I finished. If you have read this letter through to the end, I am sure you will excuse me if I have written it badly. There is no date to it, because I feel that it is safest and best for both of us that you should know nothing of where I am living. I bless you and pray for you, and bid you affectionately farewell. If you can think of me as a sister, think of me sometimes still."

Fabio sighed bitterly while he read the letter. "Why," he whispered to himself, "why does it come at such a time as this, when I cannot dare not think of her?" As he slowly folded the letter up the tears came into his eyes, and he half raised the paper to his lips. At the same moment, some one knocked at the door of the room. He started, and felt himself changing color guiltily as one of his servants entered.

"My mistress is awake," the man said, with a very grave face, and a very constrained manner; "and the gentlemen in attendance desire me to say—"

He was interrupted, before he could give his message, by one of the medical men, who had followed him into the room.

"I wish I had better news to communicate," began the doctor, gently.

"She is worse, then?" said Fabio, sinking back into the chair from which he had risen the moment before.

"She has awakened weaker instead of stronger after her sleep," returned the doctor, evasively. "I never like to give up all hope till the very last, but—"

"It is cruel not to be candid with him," interposed another voice—the voice of the doctor from Florence, who had just entered the room. "Strengthen yourself to bear the worst," he continued, addressing himself to Fabio. "She is dying. Can you compose yourself enough to go to her bedside?"

Pale and speechless, Fabio rose from his chair, and made a sign in the affirmative. He trembled so that the doctor who had first spoken was obliged to lead him out of the room.

"Your mistress has some near relations in Pisa, has she not?" said the doctor from Florence, appealing to the servant who waited near him.

"Her father, sir, Signor Luca Lomi; and her uncle, Father Rocco," answered the man. "They were here all through the day, until my mistress fell asleep."

"Do you know where to find them now?"

"Signor Luca told me he should be at his studio, and Father Rocco said I might find him at his lodgings."

"Send for them both directly. Stay, who is your mistress's confessor? He ought to be summoned without loss of time."

"My mistress's confessor is Father Rocco, sir."

"Very well—send, or go yourself, at once. Even minutes may be of importance now." Saying this, the doctor turned away, and sat down to wait for any last demands on his services, in the chair which Fabio had just left.

III

B efore the servant could get to the priest's lodgings a visitor had applied there for admission, and had been immediately received by Father Rocco himself. This favored guest was a little man, very sprucely and neatly dressed, and oppressively polite in his manner. He bowed when he first sat down, he bowed when he answered the usual inquiries about his health, and he bowed, for the third time, when Father Rocco asked what had brought him from Florence.

"Rather an awkward business," replied the little man, recovering himself uneasily after his third bow. "The dressmaker, named Nanina, whom you placed under my wife's protection about a year ago—"

"What of her?" inquired the priest eagerly.

"I regret to say she has left us, with her child-sister, and their very disagreeable dog, that growls at everybody."

"When did they go?"

"Only yesterday. I came here at once to tell you, as you were so very particular in recommending us to take care of her. It is not our fault that she has gone. My wife was kindness itself to her, and I always treated her like a duchess. I bought dinner-mats of her sister; I even put up with the thieving and growling of the disagreeable dog—"

"Where have they gone to? Have you found out that?"

"I have found out, by application at the passport-office, that they have not left Florence—but what particular part of the city they have removed to, I have not yet had time to discover."

"And pray why did they leave you, in the first place? Nanina is not a girl to do anything without a reason. She must have had some cause for going away. What was it?"

The little man hesitated, and made a fourth bow.

"You remember your private instructions to my wife and myself, when you first brought Nanina to our house?" he said, looking away rather uneasily while he spoke.

"Yes; you were to watch her, but to take care that she did not suspect you. It was just possible, at that time, that she might try to get back to Pisa without my knowing it; and everything depended on her remaining at Florence. I think, now, that I did wrong to distrust her; but it was of the last importance to provide against all possibilities, and to abstain from putting too much faith in my own good opinion of the girl. For these reasons, I certainly did instruct you to watch her privately. So far you are quite right; and I have nothing to complain of. Go on."

"You remember," resumed the little man, "that the first consequence of our following your instructions was a discovery (which we immediately communicated to you) that she was secretly learning to write?"

"Yes; and I also remember sending you word not to show that you knew what she was doing; but to wait and see if she turned her knowledge of writing to account, and took or sent any letters to the post. You informed me, in your regular monthly report, that she nearer did anything of the kind."

"Never, until three days ago; and then she was traced from her room in my house to the post-office with a letter, which she dropped into the box."

"And the address of which you discovered before she took it from your house?"

"Unfortunately I did not," answered the little man, reddening and looking askance at the priest, as if he expected to receive a severe reprimand.

But Father Rocco said nothing. He was thinking. Who could she have written to? If to Fabio, why should she have waited for months and months, after she had learned how to use her pen, before sending him a letter? If not to Fabio, to what other person could she have written?

"I regret not discovering the address—regret it most deeply," said the little man, with a low bow of apology.

"It is too late for regret," said Father Rocco, coldly. "Tell me how she came to leave your house; I have not heard that yet. Be as brief as you can. I expect to be called every moment to the bedside of a near and dear relation, who is suffering from severe illness. You shall have all my attention; but you must ask it for as short a time as possible."

"I will be briefness itself. In the first place, you must know that I have—or rather had—an idle, unscrupulous rascal of an apprentice in my business."

The priest pursed up his mouth contemptuously.

"In the second place, this same good-for-nothing fellow had the impertinence to fall in love with Nanina."

Father Rocco started, and listened eagerly.

"But I must do the girl the justice to say that she never gave him the slightest encouragement; and that, whenever he ventured to speak to her, she always quietly but very decidedly repelled him."

"A good girl!" said Father Rocco. "I always said she was a good girl. It was a mistake on my part ever to have distrusted her."

"Among the other offenses," continued the little man, "of which I now find my scoundrel of an apprentice to have been guilty, was the enormity of picking the lock of my desk, and prying into my private papers."

"You ought not to have had any. Private papers should always be burned papers."

"They shall be for the future; I will take good care of that."

"Were any of my letters to you about Nanina among these private papers?"

"Unfortunately they were. Pray, pray excuse my want of caution this time. It shall never happen again."

"Go on. Such imprudence as yours can never be excused; it can only be provided against for the future. I suppose the apprentice showed my letters to the girl?"

"I infer as much; though why he should do so—"

"Simpleton! Did you not say that he was in love with her (as you term it), and that he got no encouragement?"

"Yes; I said that—and I know it to be true."

"Well! Was it not his interest, being unable to make any impression on the girl's fancy, to establish some claim to her gratitude; and try if he could not win her that way? By showing her my letters, he would make her indebted to him for knowing that she was watched in your house. But this is not the matter in question now. You say you infer that she had seen my letters. On what grounds?"

"On the strength of this bit of paper," answered the little man, ruefully producing a note from his pocket. "She must have had your letters shown to her soon after putting her own letter into the post. For, on the evening of the same day, when I went up into her room, I found that she and her sister and the disagreeable dog had all gone, and observed this note laid on the table."

Father Rocco took the note, and read these lines:

"I have just discovered that I have been watched and
    suspected ever since my stay under your roof. It is impossible
    that I can remain another night in the house of a spy. I go

with my sister. We owe you nothing, and we are free to
live honestly where we please. If you see Father Rocco, tell
him that I can forgive his distrust of me, but that I can
never forget it. I, who had full faith in him, had a right to
expect that he should have full faith in me. It was always an
encouragement to me to think of him as a father and a friend.
I have lost that encouragement forever—and it was the last
I had left to me!

NANINA

The priest rose from his seat as he handed the note back, and the
visitor immediately followed his example.

"We must remedy this misfortune as we best may," he said, with a
sigh. "Are you ready to go back to Florence to-morrow?"

The little man bowed again.

"Find out where she is, and ascertain if she wants for anything,
and if she is living in a safe place. Say nothing about me, and make
no attempt to induce her to return to your house. Simply let me
know what you discover. The poor child has a spirit that no ordinary
people would suspect in her. She must be soothed and treated
tenderly, and we shall manage her yet. No mistakes, mind, this time!
Do just what I tell you, and do no more. Have you anything else to
say to me?"

The little man shook his head and shrugged his shoulders.

"Good-night, then," said the priest.

"Good-night," said the little man, slipping through the door that was
held open for him with the politest alacrity.

"This is vexatious," said Father Rocco, taking a turn or two in the
study after his visitor had gone. "It was bad to have done the child an
injustice—it is worse to have been found out. There is nothing for it
now but to wait till I know where she is. I like her, and I like that note
she left behind her. It is bravely, delicately, and honestly written—a
good girl—a very good girl, indeed!"

He walked to the window, breathed the fresh air for a few moments,
and quietly dismissed the subject from his mind. When he returned to
his table he had no thoughts for any one but his sick niece.

"It seems strange," he said, "that I have had no message about her yet.
Perhaps Luca has heard something. It may be well if I go to the studio
at once to find out."

He took up his hat and went to the door. Just as he opened it, Fabio's servant confronted him on the thresh old.

"I am sent to summon you to the palace," said the man. "The doctors have given up all hope."

Father Rocco turned deadly pale, and drew back a step. "Have you told my brother of this?" he asked.

"I was just on my way to the studio," answered the servant.

"I will go there instead of you, and break the bad news to him," said the priest.

They descended the stairs in silence. Just as they were about to separate at the street door, Father Rocco stopped the servant.

"How is the child?" he asked, with such sudden eagerness and impatience, that the man looked quite startled as he answered that the child was perfectly well.

"There is some consolation in that," said Father Rocco, walking away, and speaking partly to the servant, partly to himself. "My caution has misled me," he continued, pausing thoughtfully when he was left alone in the roadway. "I should have risked using the mother's influence sooner to procure the righteous restitution. All hope of compassing it now rests on the life of the child. Infant as she is, her father's ill-gotten wealth may yet be gathered back to the Church by her hands."

He proceeded rapidly on his way to the studio, until he reached the river-side and drew close to the bridge which it was necessary to cross in order to get to his brother's house. Here he stopped abruptly, as if struck by a sudden idea. The moon had just risen, and her light, streaming across the river, fell full upon his face as he stood by the parapet wall that led up to the bridge. He was so lost in thought that he did not hear the conversation of two ladies who were advancing along the pathway close behind him. As they brushed by him, the taller of the two turned round and looked back at his face.

"Father Rocco!" exclaimed the lady, stopping.

"Donna Brigida!" cried the priest, looking surprised at first, but recovering himself directly and bowing with his usual quiet politeness. "Pardon me if I thank you for honoring me by renewing our acquaintance, and then pass on to my brother's studio. A heavy affliction is likely to befall us, and I go to prepare him for it."

"You refer to the dangerous illness of your niece?" said Brigida. "I heard of it this evening. Let us hope that your fears are exaggerated, and that we may yet meet under less distressing circumstances. I have no present intention of leaving Pisa for some time, and I shall always be glad to thank Father Rocco for the politeness and consideration which he showed to me, under delicate circumstances, a year ago."

With these words she courtesied deferentially, and moved away to rejoin her friend. The priest observed that Mademoiselle Virginie lingered rather near, as if anxious to catch a few words of the conversation between Brigida and himself. Seeing this, he, in his turn, listened as the two women slowly walked away together, and heard the Italian say to her companion: "Virginie, I will lay you the price of a new dress that Fabio d'Ascoli marries again."

Father Rocco started when she said those words, as if he had trodden on fire.

"My thought!" he whispered nervously to himself. "My thought at the moment when she spoke to me! Marry again? Another wife, over whom I should have no influence! Other children, whose education would not be confided to me! What would become, then, of the restitution that I have hoped for, wrought for, prayed for?"

He stopped, and looked fixedly at the sky above him. The bridge was deserted. His black figure rose up erect, motionless, and spectral, with the white still light falling solemnly all around it. Standing so for some minutes, his first movement was to drop his hand angrily on the parapet of the bridge. He then turned round slowly in the direction by which the two women had walked away.

"Donna Brigida," he said, "I will lay you the price of fifty new dresses that Fabio d'Ascoli never marries again!"

He set his face once more toward the studio, and walked on without stopping until he arrived at the master-sculptor's door.

"Marry again?" he thought to himself, as he rang the bell. "Donna Brigida, was your first failure not enough for you? Are you going to try a second time?"

Luca Lomi himself opened the door. He drew Father Rocco hurriedly into the studio toward a single lamp burning on a stand near the partition between the two rooms.

"Have you heard anything of our poor child?" he asked. "Tell me the truth! tell me the truth at once!"

"Hush! compose yourself. I have heard," said Father Rocco, in low, mournful tones.

Luca tightened his hold on the priest's arm, and looked into his face with breathless, speechless eagerness.

"Compose yourself," repeated Father Rocco. "Compose yourself to hear the worst. My poor Luca, the doctors have given up all hope."

Luca dropped his brother's arm with a groan of despair. "Oh, Maddalena! my child—my only child!"

Reiterating these words again and again, he leaned his head against the partition and burst into tears. Sordid and coarse as his nature was, he really loved his daughter. All the heart he had was in his statues and in her.

After the first burst of his grief was exhausted, he was recalled to himself by a sensation as if some change had taken place in the lighting of the studio. He looked up directly, and dimly discerned the priest standing far down at the end of the room nearest the door, with the lamp in his hand, eagerly looking at something.

"Rocco!" he exclaimed, "Rocco, why have you taken the lamp away? What are you doing there?"

There was no movement and no answer. Luca advanced a step or two, and called again. "Rocco, what are you doing there?"

The priest heard this time, and came suddenly toward his brother, with the lamp in his hand—so suddenly that Luca started.

"What is it?" he asked, in astonishment. "Gracious God, Rocco, how pale you are!"

Still the priest never said a word. He put the lamp down on the nearest table. Luca observed that his hand shook. He had never seen his brother violently agitated before. When Rocco had announced, but a few minutes ago, that Maddalena's life was despaired of, it was in a voice which, though sorrowful, was perfectly calm. What was the meaning of this sudden panic—this strange, silent terror?

The priest observed that his brother was looking at him earnestly. "Come!" he said in a faint whisper, "come to her bedside: we have no time to lose. Get your hat, and leave it to me to put out the lamp."

He hurriedly extinguished the light while he spoke. They went down the studio side by side toward the door. The moonlight streamed through the window full on the place where the priest had been standing alone with the lamp in his hand. As they passed it, Luca felt his brother tremble, and saw him turn away his head.

Two hours later, Fabio d'Ascoli and his wife were separated in this world forever; and the servants of the palace were anticipating in whispers the order of their mistress's funeral procession to the burial-ground of the Campo Santo.

PART THIRD

I

A bout eight months after the Countess d'Ascoli had been laid in her grave in the Campo Santo, two reports were circulated through the gay world of Pisa, which excited curiosity and awakened expectation everywhere.

The first report announced that a grand masked ball was to be given at the Melani Palace, to celebrate the day on which the heir of the house attained his majority. All the friends of the family were delighted at the prospect of this festival; for the old Marquis Melani had the reputation of being one of the most hospitable, and, at the same time, one of the most eccentric men in Pisa. Every one expected, therefore, that he would secure for the entertainment of his guests, if he really gave the ball, the most whimsical novelties in the way of masks, dances, and amusements generally, that had ever been seen.

The second report was, that the rich widower, Fabio d'Ascoli, was on the point of returning to Pisa, after having improved his health and spirits by traveling in foreign countries; and that he might be expected to appear again in society, for the first time since the death of his wife, at the masked ball which was to be given in the Melani Palace. This announcement excited special interest among the young ladies of Pisa. Fabio had only reached his thirtieth year; and it was universally agreed that his return to society in his native city could indicate nothing more certainly than his desire to find a second mother for his infant child. All the single ladies would now have been ready to bet, as confidently as Brigida had offered to bet eight months before, that Fabio d'Ascoli would marry again.

For once in a way, report turned out to be true, in both the cases just mentioned. Invitations were actually issued from the Melani Palace, and Fabio returned from abroad to his home on the Arno.

In settling all the arrangements connected with his masked ball, the Marquis Melani showed that he was determined not only to deserve, but to increase, his reputation for oddity. He invented the most extravagant disguises, to be worn by some of his more intimate friends; he arranged grotesque dances, to be performed at stated periods of the evening by professional buffoons, hired from Florence. He composed a toy symphony, which included solos on every noisy plaything at that time manufactured for children's use. And not content with thus avoiding the beaten track in preparing the entertainments at the ball, he determined also to show decided originality, even in selecting the attendants who were to wait on the company. Other people in his rank of life were accustomed to employ their own and hired footmen for this purpose; the marquis resolved that his attendants should be composed of young women only; that two of his rooms should be fitted up as Arcadian bowers; and that all the prettiest girls in Pisa should be placed in them to preside over the refreshments, dressed, in accordance with the mock classical taste of the period, as shepherdesses of the time of Virgil.

The only defect of this brilliantly new idea was the difficulty of executing it. The marquis had expressly ordered that not fewer than thirty shepherdesses were to be engaged—fifteen for each bower. It would have been easy to find double this number in Pisa, if beauty had been the only quality required in the attendant damsels. But it was also absolutely necessary, for the security of the marquis's gold and silver plate, that the shepherdesses should possess, besides good looks, the very homely recommendation of a fair character. This last qualification proved, it is sad to say, to be the one small merit which the majority of the ladies willing to accept engagements at the palace did not possess. Day after day passed on; and the marquis's steward only found more and more difficulty in obtaining the appointed number of trustworthy beauties. At last his resources failed him altogether; and he appeared in his master's presence about a week before the night of the ball, to make the humiliating acknowledgment that he was entirely at his wits' end. The total number of fair shepherdesses with fair characters whom he had been able to engage amounted only to twenty-three.

"Nonsense!" cried the marquis, irritably, as soon as the steward had made his confession. "I told you to get thirty girls, and thirty I mean to have. What's the use of shaking your head when all their dresses are ordered? Thirty tunics, thirty wreaths, thirty pairs of sandals and silk stockings, thirty crooks, you scoundrel—and you have the impudence to offer me only twenty-three hands to hold them. Not a word! I won't hear a word! Get me my thirty girls, or lose your place." The marquis roared out this last terrible sentence at the top of his voice, and pointed peremptorily to the door.

The steward knew his master too well to remonstrate. He took his hat and cane, and went out. It was useless to look through the ranks of rejected volunteers again; there was not the slightest hope in that quarter. The only chance left was to call on all his friends in Pisa who had daughters out at service, and to try what he could accomplish, by bribery and persuasion, that way.

After a whole day occupied in solicitations, promises, and patient smoothing down of innumerable difficulties, the result of his efforts in the new direction was an accession of six more shepherdesses. This brought him on bravely from twenty-three to twenty-nine, and left him, at last, with only one anxiety—where was he now to find shepherdess number thirty?

He mentally asked himself that important question, as he entered a shady by-street in the neighborhood of the Campo Santo, on his way back to the Melani Palace. Sauntering slowly along in the middle of the road, and fanning himself with his handkerchief after the oppressive exertions of the day, he passed a young girl who was standing at the street door of one of the houses, apparently waiting for somebody to join her before she entered the building.

"Body of Bacchus!" exclaimed the steward (using one of those old Pagan exclaimations which survive in Italy even to the present day), "there stands the prettiest girl I have seen yet. If she would only be shepherdess number thirty, I should go home to supper with my mind at ease. I'll ask her, at any rate. Nothing can be lost by asking, and everything may be gained. Stop, my dear," he continued, seeing the girl turn to go into the house as he approached her. "Don't be afraid of me. I am steward to the Marquis Melani, and well known in Pisa as an eminently respectable man. I have something to say to you which may be greatly for your benefit. Don't look surprised; I am coming to the point at once. Do you want to earn a little money? honestly, of course. You don't look as if you were very rich, child."

"I am very poor, and very much in want of some honest work to do," answered the girl, sadly.

"Then we shall suit each other to a nicety; for I have work of the pleasantest kind to give you, and plenty of money to pay for it. But before we say anything more about that, suppose you tell me first something about yourself—who you are, and so forth. You know who I am already."

"I am only a poor work-girl, and my name is Nanina. I have nothing more, sir, to say about myself than that."

"Do you belong to Pisa?"

"Yes, sir—at least, I did. But I have been away for some time. I was a year at Florence, employed in needlework."

"All by yourself?"

"No, sir, with my little sister. I was waiting for her when you came up."

"Have you never done anything else but needlework? never been out at service?"

"Yes, sir. For the last eight months I have had a situation to wait on a lady at Florence, and my sister (who is turned eleven, sir, and can make herself very useful) was allowed to help in the nursery."

"How came you to leave this situation?"

"The lady and her family were going to Rome, sir. They would have taken me with them, but they could not take my sister. We are alone in the world, and we never have been parted from each other, and never shall be—so I was obliged to leave the situation."

"And here you are, back at Pisa—with nothing to do, I suppose?"

"Nothing yet, sir. We only came back yesterday."

"Only yesterday! You are a lucky girl, let me tell you, to have met with me. I suppose you have somebody in the town who can speak to your character?"

"The landlady of this house can, sir."

"And who is she, pray?"

"Marta Angrisani, sir."

"What! the well-known sick-nurse? You could not possibly have a better recommendation, child. I remember her being employed at the Melani Palace at the time of the marquis's last attack of gout; but I never knew that she kept a lodging-house."

"She and her daughter, sir, have owned this house longer than I can recollect. My sister and I have lived in it since I was quite a little child, and I had hoped we might be able to live here again. But the top room we used to have is taken, and the room to let lower down is far more, I am afraid, than we can afford."

"How much is it?"

Nanina mentioned the weekly rent of the room in fear and trembling. The steward burst out laughing.

"Suppose I offered you money enough to be able to take that room for a whole year at once?" he said.

Nanina looked at him in speechless amazement.

"Suppose I offered you that?" continued the steward. "And suppose

I only ask you in return to put on a fine dress and serve refreshments in a beautiful room to the company at the Marquis Melani's grand ball? What should you say to that?"

Nanina said nothing. She drew back a step or two, and looked more bewildered than before.

"You must have heard of the ball," said the steward, pompously; "the poorest people in Pisa have heard of it. It is the talk of the whole city."

Still Nanina made no answer. To have replied truthfully, she must have confessed that "the talk of the whole city" had now no interest for her. The last news from Pisa that had appealed to her sympathies was the news of the Countess d'Ascoli's death, and of Fabio's departure to travel in foreign countries. Since then she had heard nothing more of him. She was as ignorant of his return to his native city as of all the reports connected with the marquis's ball. Something in her own heart—some feeling which she had neither the desire nor the capacity to analyze—had brought her back to Pisa and to the old home which now connected itself with her tenderest recollections. Believing that Fabio was still absent, she felt that no ill motive could now be attributed to her return; and she had not been able to resist the temptation of revisiting the scene that had been associated with the first great happiness as well as with the first great sorrow of her life. Among all the poor people of Pisa, she was perhaps the very last whose curiosity could be awakened, or whose attention could be attracted by the rumor of gayeties at the Melani Palace.

But she could not confess all this; she could only listen with great humility and no small surprise, while the steward, in compassion for her ignorance, and with the hope of tempting her into accepting his offered engagement, described the arrangements of the approaching festival, and dwelt fondly on the magnificence of the Arcadian bowers, and the beauty of the shepherdesses' tunics. As soon as he had done, Nanina ventured on the confession that she should feel rather nervous in a grand dress that did not belong to her, and that she doubted very much her own capability of waiting properly on the great people at the ball. The steward, however, would hear of no objections, and called peremptorily for Marta Angrisani to make the necessary statement as to Nanina's character. While this formality was being complied with to the steward's perfect satisfaction, La Biondella came in, unaccompanied on this occasion by the usual companion of all her walks, the learned poodle Scarammuccia.

"This is Nanina's sister," said the good-natured sick-nurse, taking the first opportunity of introducing La Biondella to the great marquis's great man. "A very good, industrious little girl; and very clever at plaiting dinner-mats, in case his excellency should ever want any. What have you done with the dog, my dear?"

"I couldn't get him past the pork butcher's, three streets off," replied La Biondella. "He would sit down and look at the sausages. I am more than half afraid he means to steal some of them."

"A very pretty child," said the steward, patting La Biondella on the cheek. "We ought to have her at the hall. If his excellency should want a Cupid, or a youthful nymph, or anything small and light in that way, I shall come back and let you know. In the meantime, Nanina, consider yourself Shepherdess Number Thirty, and come to the housekeeper's room at the palace to try on your dress to-morrow. Nonsense! don't talk to me about being afraid and awkward. All you're wanted to do is to look pretty; and your glass must have told you you could do that long ago. Remember the rent of the room, my dear, and don't stand in your light and your sister's. Does the little girl like sweetmeats? Of course she does! Well, I promise you a whole box of sugar-plums to take home for her, if you will come and wait at the ball."

"Oh, go to the ball, Nanina; go to the ball!" cried La Biondella, clapping her hands.

"Of course she will go to the ball," said the nurse. "She would be mad to throw away such an excellent chance."

Nanina looked perplexed. She hesitated a little, then drew Marta Angrisani away into a corner, and whispered this question to her:

"Do you think there will be any priests at the palace where the marquis lives?"

"Heavens, child, what a thing to ask!" returned the nurse. "Priests at a masked ball! You might as well expect to find Turks performing high mass in the cathedral. But supposing you did meet with priests at the palace, what then?"

"Nothing," said Nanina, constrainedly. She turned pale, and walked away as she spoke. Her great dread, in returning to Pisa, was the dread of meeting with Father Rocco again. She had never forgotten her first discovery at Florence of his distrust of her. The bare thought of seeing him any more, after her faith in him had been shaken forever, made her feel faint and sick at heart.

WILKIE COLLINS

"To-morrow, in the housekeeper's room," said the steward, putting on his hat, "you will find your new dress all ready for you."

Nanina courtesied, and ventured on no more objections. The prospect of securing a home for a whole year to come among people whom she knew, reconciled her—influenced as she was also by Marta Angrisani's advice, and by her sister's anxiety for the promised present— to brave the trial of appearing at the ball.

"What a comfort to have it all settled at last," said the steward, as soon as he was out again in the street. "We shall see what the marquis says now. If he doesn't apologize for calling me a scoundrel the moment he sets eyes on Number Thirty, he is the most ungrateful nobleman that ever existed."

Arriving in front of the palace, the steward found workmen engaged in planning the external decorations and illuminations for the night of the ball. A little crowd had already assembled to see the ladders raised and the scaffoldings put up. He observed among them, standing near the outskirts of the throng, a lady who attracted his attention (he was an ardent admirer of the fair sex) by the beauty and symmetry of her figure. While he lingered for a moment to look at her, a shaggy poodle-dog (licking his chops, as if he had just had something to eat) trotted by, stopped suddenly close to the lady, sniffed suspiciously for an instant, and then began to growl at her without the slightest apparent provocation. The steward advancing politely with his stick to drive the dog away, saw the lady start, and heard her exclaim to herself amazedly:

"You here, you beast! Can Nanina have come back to Pisa?"

This last exclamation gave the steward, as a gallant man, an excuse for speaking to the elegant stranger.

"Excuse me, madam," he said, "but I heard you mention the name of Nanina. May I ask whether you mean a pretty little work-girl who lives near the Campo Santo?"

"The same," said the lady, looking very much surprised and interested immediately.

"It may be a gratification to you, madam, to know that she has just returned to Pisa," continued the steward, politely; "and, moreover, that she is in a fair way to rise in the world. I have just engaged her to wait at the marquis's grand ball, and I need hardly say, under those circumstances, that if she plays her cards properly her fortune is made."

The lady bowed, looked at her informant very intently and thoughtfully for a moment, then suddenly walked away without uttering a word.

"A curious woman," thought the steward, entering the palace. "I must ask Number Thirty about her to-morrow."

II

The death of Maddalena d'Ascoli produced a complete change in the lives of her father and her uncle. After the first shock of the bereavement was over, Luca Lomi declared that it would be impossible for him to work in his studio again—for some time to come at least—after the death of the beloved daughter, with whom every corner of it was now so sadly and closely associated. He accordingly accepted an engagement to assist in restoring several newly discovered works of ancient sculpture at Naples, and set forth for that city, leaving the care of his work-rooms at Pisa entirely to his brother.

On the master-sculptor's departure, Father Rocco caused the statues and busts to be carefully enveloped in linen cloths, locked the studio doors, and, to the astonishment of all who knew of his former industry and dexterity as a sculptor, never approached the place again. His clerical duties he performed with the same assiduity as ever; but he went out less than had been his custom hitherto to the houses of his friends. His most regular visits were to the Ascoli Palace, to inquire at the porter's lodge after the health of Maddalena's child, who was always reported to be thriving admirably under the care of the best nurses that could be found in Pisa. As for any communications with his polite little friend from Florence, they had ceased months ago. The information—speedily conveyed to him—that Nanina was in the service of one of the most respectable ladies in the city seemed to relieve any anxieties which he might otherwise have felt on her account. He made no attempt to justify himself to her; and only required that his over-courteous little visitor of former days should let him know whenever the girl might happen to leave her new situation.

The admirers of Father Rocco, seeing the alteration in his life, and the increased quietness of his manner, said that, as he was growing older, he was getting more and more above the things of this world. His enemies (for even Father Rocco had them) did not scruple to assert that the change in him was decidedly for the worse, and that he belonged to the order of men who are most to be distrusted when they become most subdued. The priest himself paid no attention either to his eulogists or his depreciators. Nothing disturbed the regularity and discipline of his daily habits; and vigilant Scandal, though she sought often to surprise him, sought always in vain.

Such was Father Rocco's life from the period of his niece's death to Fabio's return to Pisa.

As a matter of course, the priest was one of the first to call at the palace and welcome the young nobleman back. What passed between them at this interview never was precisely known; but it was surmised readily enough that some misunderstanding had taken place, for Father Rocco did not repeat his visit. He made no complaints of Fabio, but simply stated that he had said something, intended for the young man's good, which had not been received in a right spirit; and that he thought it desirable to avoid the painful chance of any further collision by not presenting himself at the palace again for some little time. People were rather amazed at this. They would have been still more surprised if the subject of the masked ball had not just then occupied all their attention, and prevented their noticing it, by another strange event in connection with the priest. Father Rocco, some weeks after the cessation of his intercourse with Fabio, returned one morning to his old way of life as a sculptor, and opened the long-closed doors of his brother's studio.

Luca Lomi's former workmen, discovering this, applied to him immediately for employment; but were informed that their services would not be needed. Visitors called at the studio, but were always sent away again by the disappointing announcement that there was nothing new to show them. So the days passed on until Nanina left her situation and returned to Pisa. This circumstance was duly reported to Father Rocco by his correspondent at Florence; but, whether he was too much occupied among the statues, or whether it was one result of his cautious resolution never to expose himself unnecessarily to so much as the breath of detraction, he made no attempt to see Nanina, or even to justify himself toward her by writing her a letter. All his mornings continued to be spent alone in the studio, and all his afternoons to be occupied by his clerical duties, until the day before the masked ball at the Melani Palace.

Early on that day he covered over the statues, and locked the doors of the work-rooms once more; then returned to his own lodgings, and did not go out again. One or two of his friends who wanted to see him were informed that he was not well enough to be able to receive them. If they had penetrated into his little study, and had seen him, they would have been easily satisfied that this was no mere excuse. They would have noticed that his face was startlingly pale, and that the ordinary composure of his manner was singularly disturbed.

Toward evening this restlessness increased, and his old housekeeper, on pressing him to take some nourishment, was astonished to hear him answer her sharply and irritably, for the first time since she had been in his service. A little later her surprise was increased by his sending her with a note to the Ascoli Palace, and by the quick return of an answer, brought ceremoniously by one of Fabio's servants. "It is long since he has had any communication with that quarter. Are they going to be friends again?" thought the housekeeper as she took the answer upstairs to her master.

"I feel better to-night," he said as he read it; "well enough indeed to venture out. If any one inquires for me, tell them that I am gone to the Ascoli Palace." Saying this, he walked to the door; then returned, and trying the lock of his cabinet, satisfied himself that it was properly secured; then went out.

He found Fabio in one of the large drawing-rooms of the palace, walking irritably backward and forward, with several little notes crumpled together in his hands, and a plain black domino dress for the masquerade of the ensuing night spread out on one of the tables.

"I was just going to write to you," said the young man, abruptly, "when I received your letter. You offer me a renewal of our friendship, and I accept the offer. I have no doubt those references of yours, when we last met, to the subject of second marriages were well meant, but they irritated me; and, speaking under that irritation, I said words that I had better not have spoken. If I pained you, I am sorry for it. Wait! pardon me for one moment. I have not quite done yet. It seems that you are by no means the only person in Pisa to whom the question of my possibly marrying again appears to have presented itself. Ever since it was known that I intended to renew my intercourse with society at the ball to-morrow night, I have been persecuted by anonymous letters—infamous letters, written from some motive which it is impossible for me to understand. I want your advice on the best means of discovering the writers; and I have also a very important question to ask you. But read one of the letters first yourself; any one will do as a sample of the rest."

Fixing his eyes searchingly on the priest, he handed him one of the notes. Still a little paler than usual, Father Rocco sat down by the nearest lamp, and shading his eyes, read these lines:

"COUNT FABIO—It is the common talk of Pisa that you are likely, as a young man left with a motherless child, to marry again. Your having accepted an invitation to the Melani Palace gives a color of truth to this report. Widowers who are true to the departed do not go among all the handsomest single women in a city at a masked ball. Reconsider your determination, and remain at home. I know you, and I knew your wife, and I say to you solemnly, avoid temptation, for you must never marry again. Neglect my advice and you will repent it to the end of your life. I have reasons for what I say—serious, fatal reasons, which I cannot divulge. If you would let your wife lie easy in her grave, if you would avoid a terrible warning, go not to the masked ball!"

"I ask you, and I ask any man, if that is not infamous?" exclaimed Fabio, passionately, as the priest handed him back the letter. "An attempt to work on my fears through the memory of my poor dead wife! An insolent assumption that I want to marry again, when I myself have not even so much as thought of the subject at all! What is the secret object of this letter, and of the rest here that resemble it? Whose interest is it to keep me away from the ball? What is the meaning of such a phrase as, 'If you would let your wife lie easy in her grave'? Have you no advice to give me—no plan to propose for discovering the vile hand that traced these lines? Speak to me! Why, in Heaven's name, don't you speak?"

The priest leaned his head on his hand, and, turning his face from the light as if it dazzled his eyes, replied in his lowest and quietest tones:

"I cannot speak till I have had time to think. The mystery of that letter is not to be solved in a moment. There are things in it that are enough to perplex and amaze any man!"

"What things?"

"It is impossible for me to go into details—at least at the present moment."

"You speak with a strange air of secrecy. Have you nothing definite to say—no advice to give me?"

"I should advise you not to go to the ball."

"You would! Why?"

"If I gave you my reasons, I am afraid I should only be irritating you to no purpose."

"Father Rocco, neither your words nor your manner satisfy me. You speak in riddles; and you sit there in the dark with your face hidden from me—"

The priest instantly started up and turned his face to the light.

"I recommend you to control your temper, and to treat me with common courtesy," he said, in his quietest, firmest tones, looking at Fabio steadily while he spoke.

"We will not prolong this interview," said the young man, calming himself by an evident effort. "I have one question to ask you, and then no more to say."

The priest bowed his head, in token that he was ready to listen. He still stood up, calm, pale, and firm, in the full light of the lamp.

"It is just possible," continued Fabio, "that these letters may refer to some incautious words which my late wife might have spoken. I ask you as her spiritual director, and as a near relation who enjoyed her confidence, if you ever heard her express a wish, in the event of my surviving her, that I should abstain from marrying again?"

"Did she never express such a wish to you?"

"Never. But why do you evade my question by asking me another?"

"It is impossible for me to reply to your question."

"For what reason?"

"Because it is impossible for me to give answers which must refer, whether they are affirmative or negative, to what I have heard in confession."

"We have spoken enough," said Fabio, turning angrily from the priest. "I expected you to help me in clearing up these mysteries, and you do your best to thicken them. What your motives are, what your conduct means, it is impossible for me to know, but I say to you, what I would say in far other terms, if they were here, to the villains who have written these letters—no menaces, no mysteries, no conspiracies, will prevent me from being at the ball to-morrow. I can listen to persuasion, but I scorn threats. There lies my dress for the masquerade; no power on earth shall prevent me from wearing it to-morrow night!" He pointed, as he spoke, to the black domino and half-mask lying on the table.

"No power on *earth!*" repeated Father Rocco, with a smile, and an emphasis on the last word. "Superstitious still, Count Fabio! Do you suspect the powers of the other world of interfering with mortals at masquerades?"

Fabio started, and, turning from the table, fixed his eyes intently on the priest's face.

"You suggested just now that we had better not prolong this interview," said Father Rocco, still smiling. "I think you were right; if we part at once, we may still part friends. You have had my advice not to go to the ball, and you decline following it. I have nothing more to say. Good-night."

Before Fabio could utter the angry rejoinder that rose to his lips, the door of the room had opened and closed again, and the priest was gone.

III

The next night, at the time of assembling specified in the invitations to the masked ball, Fabio was still lingering in his palace, and still allowing the black domino to lie untouched and unheeded on his dressing-table. This delay was not produced by any change in his resolution to go to the Melani Palace. His determination to be present at the ball remained unshaken; and yet, at the last moment, he lingered and lingered on, without knowing why. Some strange influence seemed to be keeping him within the walls of his lonely home. It was as if the great, empty, silent palace had almost recovered on that night the charm which it had lost when its mistress died.

He left his own apartment and went to the bedroom where his infant child lay asleep in her little crib. He sat watching her, and thinking quietly and tenderly of many past events in his life for a long time, then returned to his room. A sudden sense of loneliness came upon him after his visit to the child's bedside; but he did not attempt to raise his spirits even then by going to the ball. He descended instead to his study, lighted his reading-lamp, and then, opening a bureau, took from one of the drawers in it the letter which Nanina had written to him. This was not the first time that a sudden sense of his solitude had connected itself inexplicably with the remembrance of the work-girl's letter.

He read it through slowly, and when he had done, kept it open in his hand. "I have youth, titles, wealth," he thought to himself, sadly; "everything that is sought after in this world. And yet if I try to think of any human being who really and truly loves me, I can remember but one—the poor, faithful girl who wrote these lines!"

Old recollections of the first day when he met with Nanina, of the first sitting she had given him in Luca Lomi's studio, of the first visit to the neat little room in the by-street, began to rise more and more vividly in his mind. Entirely absorbed by them, he sat absently drawing with pen and ink, on some sheets of letter-paper lying under his hand, lines and circles, and fragments of decorations, and vague remembrances of old ideas for statues, until the sudden sinking of the flame of his lamp awoke his attention abruptly to present things.

He looked at his watch. It was close on midnight.

This discovery at last aroused him to the necessity of immediate departure. In a few minutes he had put on his domino and mask, and was on his way to the ball.

Before he reached the Melani Palace the first part of the entertainment had come to an end. The "Toy Symphony" had been played, the grotesque dance performed, amid universal laughter; and now the guests were, for the most part, fortifying themselves in the Arcadian bowers for new dances, in which all persons present were expected to take part. The Marquis Melani had, with characteristic oddity, divided his two classical refreshment-rooms into what he termed the Light and Heavy Departments. Fruit, pastry, sweetmeats, salads, and harmless drinks were included under the first head, and all the stimulating liquors and solid eatables under the last. The thirty shepherdesses had been, according to the marquis's order, equally divided at the outset of the evening between the two rooms. But as the company began to crowd more and more resolutely in the direction of the Heavy Department, ten of the shepherdesses attached to the Light Department were told off to assist in attending on the hungry and thirsty majority of guests who were not to be appeased by pastry and lemonade. Among the five girls who were left behind in the room for the light refreshments was Nanina. The steward soon discovered that the novelty of her situation made her really nervous, and he wisely concluded that if he trusted her where the crowd was greatest and the noise loudest, she would not only be utterly useless, but also very much in the way of her more confident and experienced companions.

When Fabio arrived at the palace, the jovial uproar in the Heavy Department was at its height, and several gentlemen, fired by the classical costumes of the shepherdesses, were beginning to speak Latin to them with a thick utterance, and a valorous contempt for all restrictions of gender, number, and case. As soon as he could escape from the congratulations on his return to his friends, which poured on him from all sides, Fabio withdrew to seek some quieter room. The heat, noise, and confusion had so bewildered him, after the tranquil life he had been leading for many months past, that it was quite a relief to stroll through the half deserted dancing-rooms, to the opposite extremity of the great suite of apartments, and there to find himself in a second Arcadian bower, which seemed peaceful enough to deserve its name.

A few guests were in this room when he first entered it, but the distant sound of some first notes of dance music drew them all away. After a careless look at the quaint decorations about him, he sat down alone on a divan near the door, and beginning already to feel the heat and discomfort of his mask, took it off. He had not removed it more than a moment before he heard a faint cry in the direction of a long refreshment-table, behind which the five waiting-girls were standing. He started up directly, and could hardly believe his senses, when he found himself standing face to face with Nanina.

Her cheeks had turned perfectly colorless. Her astonishment at seeing the young nobleman appeared to have some sensation of terror mingled with it. The waiting-woman who happened to stand by her side instinctively stretched out an arm to support her, observing that she caught at the edge of the table as Fabio hurried round to get behind it and speak to her. When he drew near, her head drooped on her breast, and she said, faintly: "I never knew you were at Pisa; I never thought you would be here. Oh, I am true to what I said in my letter, though I seem so false to it!"

"I want to speak to you about the letter—to tell you how carefully I have kept it, how often I have read it," said Fabio.

She turned away her head, and tried hard to repress the tears that would force their way into her eyes "We should never have met," she said; "never, never have met again!"

Before Fabio could reply, the waiting-woman by Nanina's side interposed.

"For Heaven's sake, don't stop speaking to her here!" she exclaimed, impatiently. "If the steward or one of the upper servants was to come in, you would get her into dreadful trouble. Wait till to-morrow, and find some fitter place than this."

Fabio felt the justice of the reproof immediately. He tore a leaf out of his pocketbook, and wrote on it, "I must tell you how I honor and thank you for that letter. To-morrow—ten o'clock—the wicket-gate at the back of the Ascoli gardens. Believe in my truth and honor, Nanina, for I believe implicitly in yours." Having written these lines, he took from among his bunch of watch-seals a little key, wrapped it up in the note, and pressed it into her hand. In spite of himself his fingers lingered round hers, and he was on the point of speaking to her again, when he saw the waiting-woman's hand, which was just raised to motion him away, suddenly drop. Her color changed at the same moment, and she looked fixedly across the table.

He turned round immediately, and saw a masked woman standing alone in the room, dressed entirely in yellow from head to foot. She had a yellow hood, a yellow half-mask with deep fringe hanging down over her mouth, and a yellow domino, cut at the sleeves and edges into long flame-shaped points, which waved backward and forward tremulously in the light air wafted through the doorway. The woman's black eyes seemed to gleam with an evil brightness through the sight-holes of the mask, and the tawny fringe hanging before her mouth fluttered slowly with every breath she drew. Without a word or a gesture she stood before the table, and her gleaming black eyes fixed steadily on Fabio the instant he confronted her. A sudden chill struck through him, as he observed that the yellow of the stranger's domino and mask was of precisely the same shade as the yellow of the hangings and furniture which his wife had chosen after their marriage for the decoration of her favorite sitting-room.

"The Yellow Mask!" whispered the waiting-girls nervously, crowding together behind the table. "The Yellow Mask again!"

"Make her speak!"

"Ask her to have something!"

"This gentleman will ask her. Speak to her, sir. Do speak to her! She glides about in that fearful yellow dress like a ghost."

Fabio looked around mechanically at the girl who was whispering to him. He saw at the same time that Nanina still kept her head turned away, and that she had her handkerchief at her eyes. She was evidently struggling yet with the agitation produced by their unexpected meeting, and was, most probably for that reason, the only person in the room not conscious of the presence of the Yellow Mask.

"Speak to her, sir. Do speak to her!" whispered two of the waiting-girls together.

Fabio turned again toward the table. The black eyes were still gleaming at him from behind the tawny yellow of the mask. He nodded to the girls who had just spoken, cast one farewell look at Nanina, and moved down the room to get round to the side of the table at which the Yellow Mask was standing. Step by step as he moved the bright eyes followed him. Steadily and more steadily their evil light seemed to shine through and through him, as he turned the corner of the table and approached the still, spectral figure.

He came close up to the woman, but she never moved; her eyes never wavered for an instant. He stopped and tried to speak; but the chill struck through him again. An overpowering dread, an unutterable loathing seized on him; all sense of outer things—the whispering of the waiting-girls behind the table, the gentle cadence of the dance music, the distant hum of joyous talk—suddenly left him. He turned away shuddering, and quitted the room.

Following the sound of the music, and desiring before all things now to join the crowd wherever it was largest, he was stopped in one of the smaller apartments by a gentleman who had just risen from the card table, and who held out his hand with the cordiality of an old friend.

"Welcome back to the world, Count Fabio!" he began, gayly, then suddenly checked himself. "Why, you look pale, and your hand feels cold. Not ill, I hope?"

"No, no. I have been rather startled—I can't say why—by a very strangely dressed woman, who fairly stared me out of countenance."

"You don't mean the Yellow Mask?"

"Yes I do. Have you seen her?"

"Everybody has seen her; but nobody can make her unmask, or get her to speak. Our host has not the slightest notion who she is; and our hostess is horribly frightened at her. For my part, I think she has given us quite enough of her mystery and her grim dress; and if my name, instead of being nothing but plain Andrea D'Arbino, was Marquis Melani, I would say to her: 'Madam, we are here to laugh and amuse ourselves; suppose you open your lips, and charm us by appearing in a prettier dress!'"

During this conversation they had sat down together, with their backs toward the door, by the side of one of the card-tables. While D'Arbino was speaking, Fabio suddenly felt himself shuddering again, and became conscious of a sound of low breathing behind him.

He turned round instantly, and there, standing between them, and peering down at them, was the Yellow Mask!

Fabio started up, and his friend followed his example. Again the gleaming black eyes rested steadily on the young nobleman's face, and again their look chilled him to the heart.

"Yellow Lady, do you know my friend?" exclaimed D'Arbino, with mock solemnity.

There was no answer. The fatal eyes never moved from Fabio's face.

"Yellow Lady," continued the other, "listen to the music. Will you dance with me?"

The eyes looked away, and the figure glided slowly from the room.

"My dear count," said D'Arbino, "that woman seems to have quite an effect on you. I declare she has left you paler than ever. Come into the supper-room with me, and have some wine; you really look as if you wanted it."

They went at once to the large refreshment-room. Nearly all the guests had by this time begun to dance again. They had the whole apartment, therefore, almost entirely to themselves.

Among the decorations of the room, which were not strictly in accordance with genuine Arcadian simplicity, was a large looking-glass, placed over a well-furnished sideboard. D'Arbino led Fabio in this direction, exchanging greetings as he advanced with a gentleman who stood near the glass looking into it, and carelessly fanning himself with his mask.

"My dear friend!" cried D'Arbino, "you are the very man to lead us straight to the best bottle of wine in the palace. Count Fabio, let me present to you my intimate and good friend, the Cavaliere Finello, with whose family I know you are well acquainted. Finello, the count is a little out of spirits, and I have prescribed a good dose of wine. I see a whole row of bottles at your side, and I leave it to you to apply the remedy. Glasses there! three glasses, my lovely shepherdess with the black eyes— the three largest you have got."

The glasses were brought; the Cavaliere Finello chose a particular bottle, and filled them. All three gentlemen turned round to the sideboard to use it as a table, and thus necessarily faced the looking-glass.

"Now let us drink the toast of toasts," said D'Arbino. "Finello, Count Fabio—the ladies of Pisa!"

Fabio raised the wine to his lips, and was on the point of drinking it, when he saw reflected in the glass the figure of the Yellow Mask. The glittering eyes were again fixed on him, and the yellow-hooded head bowed slowly, as if in acknowledgment of the toast he was about to drink. For the third time the strange chill seized him, and he set down his glass of wine untasted.

"What is the matter?" asked D'Arbino.

"Have you any dislike, count, to that particular wine?" inquired the cavaliere.

"The Yellow Mask!" whispered Fabio. "The Yellow Mask again!"

They all three turned round directly toward the door. But it was too late—the figure had disappeared.

WILKIE COLLINS

"Does any one know who this Yellow Mask is?" asked Finello. "One may guess by the walk that the figure is a woman's. Perhaps it may be the strange color she has chosen for her dress, or perhaps her stealthy way of moving from room to room; but there is certainly something mysterious and startling about her."

"Startling enough, as the count would tell you," said D'Arbino. "The Yellow Mask has been responsible for his loss of spirits and change of complexion, and now she has prevented him even from drinking his wine."

"I can't account for it," said Fabio, looking round him uneasily; "but this is the third room into which she has followed me—the third time she has seemed to fix her eyes on me alone. I suppose my nerves are hardly in a fit state yet for masked balls and adventures; the sight of her seems to chill me. Who can she be?"

"If she followed me a fourth time," said Finello, "I should insist on her unmasking."

"And suppose she refused?" asked his friend

"Then I should take her mask off for her."

"It is impossible to do that with a woman," said Fabio. "I prefer trying to lose her in the crowd. Excuse me, gentlemen, if I leave you to finish the wine, and then to meet me, if you like, in the great ballroom."

He retired as he spoke, put on his mask, and joined the dancers immediately, taking care to keep always in the most crowded corner of the apartment. For some time this plan of action proved successful, and he saw no more of the mysterious yellow domino. Ere long, however, some new dances were arranged, in which the great majority of the persons in the ballroom took part; the figures resembling the old English country dances in this respect, that the ladies and gentlemen were placed in long rows opposite to each other. The sets consisted of about twenty couples each, placed sometimes across, and sometimes along the apartment; and the spectators were all required to move away on either side, and range themselves close to the walls. As Fabio among others complied with this necessity, he looked down a row of dancers waiting during the performance of the orchestral prelude; and there, watching him again, from the opposite end of the lane formed by the gentlemen on one side and the ladies on the other, he saw the Yellow Mask.

He moved abruptly back, toward another row of dancers, placed at right angles to the first row; and there again; at the opposite end of the gay lane of brightly-dressed figures, was the Yellow Mask. He slipped into the middle of the room, but it was only to find her occupying his former position near the wall, and still, in spite of his disguise, watching him through row after row of dancers. The persecution began to grow intolerable; he felt a kind of angry curiosity mingling now with the vague dread that had hitherto oppressed him. Finello's advice recurred to his memory; and he determined to make the woman unmask at all hazards. With this intention he returned to the supper-room in which he had left his friends.

They were gone, probably to the ballroom, to look for him. Plenty of wine was still left on the sideboard, and he poured himself out a glass. Finding that his hand trembled as he did so, he drank several more glasses in quick succession, to nerve himself for the approaching encounter with the Yellow Mask. While he was drinking he expected every moment to see her in the looking-glass again; but she never appeared—and yet he felt almost certain that he had detected her gliding out after him when he left the ballroom.

He thought it possible that she might be waiting for him in one of the smaller apartments, and, taking off his mask, walked through several of them without meeting her, until he came to the door of the refreshment-room in which Nanina and he had recognized each other. The waiting-woman behind the table, who had first spoken to him, caught sight of him now, and ran round to the door.

"Don't come in and speak to Nanina again," she said, mistaking the purpose which had brought him to the door. "What with frightening her first, and making her cry afterward, you have rendered her quite unfit for her work. The steward is in there at this moment, very good-natured, but not very sober. He says she is pale and red-eyed, and not fit to be a shepherdess any longer, and that, as she will not be missed now, she may go home if she likes. We have got her an old cloak, and she is going to try and slip through the rooms unobserved, to get downstairs and change her dress. Don't speak to her, pray, or you will only make her cry again; and what is worse, make the steward fancy—"

She stopped at that last word, and pointed suddenly over Fabio's shoulder.

"The Yellow Mask!" she exclaimed. "Oh, sir, draw her away into the ballroom, and give Nanina a chance of getting out!"

Fabio turned directly, and approached the Mask, who, as they looked at each other, slowly retreated before him. The waiting-woman, seeing the yellow figure retire, hastened back to Nanina in the refreshment-room.

Slowly the masked woman retreated from one apartment to another till she entered a corridor brilliantly lighted up and beautifully ornamented with flowers. On the right hand this corridor led to the ballroom; on the left to an ante-chamber at the head of the palace staircase. The Yellow Mask went on a few paces toward the left, then stopped. The bright eyes fixed themselves as before on Fabio's face, but only for a moment. He heard a light step behind him, and then he saw the eyes move. Following the direction they took, he turned round, and discovered Nanina, wrapped up in the old cloak which was to enable her to get downstairs unobserved.

"Oh, how can I get out? how can I get out?" cried the girl, shrinking back affrightedly as she saw the Yellow Mask.

"That way," said Fabio, pointing in the direction of the ballroom. "Nobody will notice you in the cloak; it will only be thought some new disguise." He took her arm as he spoke, to reassure her, and continued in a whisper, "Don't forget to-morrow."

At the same moment he felt a hand laid on him. It was the hand of the masked woman, and it put him back from Nanina.

In spite of himself, he trembled at her touch, but still retained presence of mind enough to sign to the girl to make her escape. With a look of eager inquiry in the direction of the mask, and a half suppressed exclamation of terror, she obeyed him, and hastened away toward the ballroom.

"We are alone," said Fabio, confronting the gleaming black eyes, and reaching out his hand resolutely toward the Yellow Mask. "Tell me who you are, and why you follow me, or I will uncover your face, and solve the mystery for myself."

The woman pushed his hand aside, and drew back a few paces, but never spoke a word. He followed her. There was not an instant to be lost, for just then the sound of footsteps hastily approaching the corridor became audible.

"Now or never," he whispered to himself, and snatched at the mask.

His arm was again thrust aside; but this time the woman raised her disengaged hand at the same moment, and removed the yellow mask.

The lamps shed their soft light full on her face.

It was the face of his dead wife.

IV

S ignor Andrea D'Arbino, searching vainly through the various rooms in the palace for Count Fabio d'Ascoli, and trying as a last resource, the corridor leading to the ballroom and grand staircase, discovered his friend lying on the floor in a swoon, without any living creature near him. Determining to avoid alarming the guests, if possible, D'Arbino first sought help in the antechamber. He found there the marquis's valet, assisting the Cavaliere Finello (who was just taking his departure) to put on his cloak.

While Finello and his friend carried Fabio to an open window in the antechamber, the valet procured some iced water. This simple remedy, and the change of atmosphere, proved enough to restore the fainting man to his senses, but hardly—as it seemed to his friends—to his former self. They noticed a change to blankness and stillness in his face, and when he spoke, an indescribable alteration in the tone of his voice.

"I found you in a room in the corridor," said D'Arbino. "What made you faint? Don't you remember? Was it the heat?"

Fabio waited for a moment, painfully collecting his ideas. He looked at the valet, and Finello signed to the man to withdraw.

"Was it the heat?" repeated D'Arbino.

"No," answered Fabio, in strangely hushed, steady tones. "I have seen the face that was behind the yellow mask."

"Well?"

"It was the face of my dead wife."

"Your dead wife!"

"When the mask was removed I saw her face. Not as I remember it in the pride of her youth and beauty—not even as I remember her on her sick-bed—but as I remember her in her coffin."

"Count! for God's sake, rouse yourself! Collect your thoughts—remember where you are—and free your mind of its horrible delusion."

"Spare me all remonstrances; I am not fit to bear them. My life has only one object now—the pursuing of this mystery to the end. Will you help me? I am scarcely fit to act for myself."

He still spoke in the same unnaturally hushed, deliberate tones. D'Arbino and Finello exchanged glances behind him as he rose from the sofa on which he had hitherto been lying.

"We will help you in everything," said D'Arbino, soothingly. "Trust in us to the end. What do you wish to do first?"

"The figure must have gone through this room. Let us descend the staircase and ask the servants if they have seen it pass."

(Both D'Arbino and Finello remarked that he did not say *her*.)

They inquired down to the very courtyard. Not one of the servants had seen the Yellow Mask.

The last resource was the porter at the outer gate. They applied to him; and in answer to their questions he asserted that he had most certainly seen a lady in a yellow domino and mask drive away, about half an hour before, in a hired coach.

"Should you remember the coachman again?" asked D'Arbino.

"Perfectly; he is an old friend of mine."

"And you know where he lives?"

"Yes; as well as I know where I do."

"Any reward you like, if you can get somebody to mind your lodge, and can take us to that house."

In a few minutes they were following the porter through the dark, silent streets. "We had better try the stables first," said the man. "My friend, the coachman, will hardly have had time to do more than set the lady down. We shall most likely catch him just putting up his horses."

The porter turned out to be right. On entering the stable-yard, they found that the empty coach had just driven into it.

"You have been taking home a lady in a yellow domino from the masquerade?" said D'Arbino, putting some money into the coachman's hand.

"Yes, sir; I was engaged by that lady for the evening—engaged to drive her to the ball as well as to drive her home."

"Where did you take her from?"

"From a very extraordinary place—from the gate of the Campo Santo burial-ground."

During this colloquy, Finello and D'Arbino had been standing with Fabio between them, each giving him an arm. The instant the last answer was given, he reeled back with a cry of horror.

"Where have you taken her to now?" asked D'Arbino. He looked about him nervously as he put the question, and spoke for the first time in a whisper.

"To the Campo Santo again," said the coachman.

Fabio suddenly drew his arms out of the arms of his friends, and sank to his knees on the ground, hiding his face. From some broken exclaimations which escaped him, it seemed as if he dreaded that his senses were leaving him, and that he was praying to be preserved in his right mind.

"Why is he so violently agitated?" said Finello, eagerly, to his friend.

"Hush!" returned the other. "You heard him say that when he saw the face behind the yellow mask, it was the face of his dead wife?"

"Yes. But what then?"

"His wife was buried in the Campo Santo."

V

Of all the persons who had been present, in any capacity, at the Marquis Melani's ball, the earliest riser on the morning after it was Nanina. The agitation produced by the strange events in which she had been concerned destroyed the very idea of sleep. Through the hours of darkness she could not even close her eyes; and, as soon as the new day broke, she rose to breathe the early morning air at her window, and to think in perfect tranquillity over all that had passed since she entered the Melani Palace to wait on the guests at the masquerade.

On reaching home the previous night, all her other sensations had been absorbed in a vague feeling of mingled dread and curiosity, produced by the sight of the weird figure in the yellow mask, which she had left standing alone with Fabio in the palace corridor. The morning light, however, suggested new thoughts. She now opened the note which the young nobleman had pressed into her hand, and read over and over again the hurried pencil lines scrawled on the paper. Could there be any harm, any forgetfulness of her own duty, in using the key inclosed in the note, and keeping her appointment in the Ascoli gardens at ten o'clock? Surely not—surely the last sentence he had written, "Believe in my truth and honor, Nanina, for I believe implicitly in yours," was enough to satisfy her this time that she could not be doing wrong in listening for once to the pleading of her own heart. And besides, there in her lap lay the key of the wicket-gate. It was absolutely necessary to use that, if only for the purpose of giving it back safely into the hand of its owner.

As this last thought was passing through her mind, and plausibly overcoming any faint doubts and difficulties which she might still have left, she was startled by a sudden knocking at the street door; and, looking out of the window immediately, saw a man in livery standing in the street, anxiously peering up at the house to see if his knocking had aroused anybody.

"Does Marta Angrisani, the sick-nurse, live here?" inquired the man, as soon as Nanina showed herself at the window.

"Yes," she answered. "Must I call her up? Is there some person ill?"

"Call her up directly," said the servant; "she is wanted at the Ascoli Palace. My master, Count Fabio—"

Nanina waited to hear no more. She flew to the room in which the sick-nurse slept, and awoke her, almost roughly, in an instant.

"He is ill!" she cried, breathlessly. "Oh, make haste, make haste! He is ill, and he has sent for you!"

Marta inquired who had sent for her, and on being informed, promised to lose no time. Nanina ran downstairs to tell the servant that the sick-nurse was getting on her clothes. The man's serious expression, when she came close to him, terrified her. All her usual self-distrust vanished; and she entreated him, without attempting to conceal her anxiety, to tell her particularly what his master's illness was, and how it had affected him so suddenly after the ball.

"I know nothing about it," answered the man, noticing Nanina's manner as she put her question, with some surprise, "except that my master was brought home by two gentlemen, friends of his, about a couple of hours ago, in a very sad state; half out of his mind, as it seemed to me. I gathered from what was said that he had got a dreadful shock from seeing some woman take off her mask, and show her face to him at the ball. How that could be I don't in the least understand; but I know that when the doctor was sent for, he looked very serious, and talked about fearing brain-fever."

Here the servant stopped; for, to his astonishment, he saw Nanina suddenly turn away from him, and then heard her crying bitterly as she went back into the house.

Marta Angrisani had huddled on her clothes and was looking at herself in the glass to see that she was sufficiently presentable to appear at the palace, when she felt two arms flung round her neck; and, before she could say a word, found Nanina sobbing on her bosom.

"He is ill—he is in danger!" cried the girl. "I must go with you to help him. You have always been kind to me, Marta—be kinder than ever now. Take me with you—take me with you to the palace!"

"You, child!" exclaimed the nurse, gently unclasping her arms.

"Yes—yes! if it is only for an hour," pleaded Nanina; "if it is only for one little hour every day. You have only to say that I am your helper, and they would let me in. Marta! I shall break my heart if I can't see him, and help him to get well again."

The nurse still hesitated. Nanina clasped her round the neck once more, and laid her cheek—burning hot now, though the tears had been streaming down it but an instant before—close to the good woman's face.

"I love him, Marta; great as he is, I love him with all my heart and soul and strength," she went on, in quick, eager, whispering tones; "and he loves me. He would have married me if I had not gone away to save him from it. I could keep my love for him a secret while he was well; I could stifle it, and crush it down, and wither it up by absence. But now he is ill, it gets beyond me; I can't master it. Oh, Marta! don't break my heart by denying me! I have suffered so much for his sake, that I have earned the right to nurse him!"

Marta was not proof against this last appeal. She had one great and rare merit for a middle-aged woman—she had not forgotten her own youth.

"Come, child," said she, soothingly; "I won't attempt to deny you. Dry your eyes, put on your mantilla; and, when we get face to face with the doctor, try to look as old and ugly as you can, if you want to be let into the sick-room along with me."

The ordeal of medical scrutiny was passed more easily than Marta Angrisani had anticipated. It was of great importance, in the doctor's opinion, that the sick man should see familiar faces at his bedside. Nanina had only, therefore, to state that he knew her well, and that she had sat to him as a model in the days when he was learning the art of sculpture, to be immediately accepted as Marta's privileged assistant in the sick-room.

The worst apprehensions felt by the doctor for the patient were soon realized. The fever flew to his brain. For nearly six weeks he lay prostrate, at the mercy of death; now raging with the wild strength of delirium, and now sunk in the speechless, motionless, sleepless exhaustion which was his only repose. At last; the blessed day came when he enjoyed his first sleep, and when the doctor began, for the first time, to talk of the future with hope. Even then, however, the same terrible peculiarity marked his light dreams which had previously shown itself in his fierce delirium. From the faintly uttered, broken phrases which dropped from him when he slept, as from the wild words which burst from him when his senses were deranged, the one sad discovery inevitably resulted— that his mind was still haunted, day and night, hour after hour, by the figure in the yellow mask.

As his bodily health improved, the doctor in attendance on him grew more and more anxious as to the state of his mind. There was no appearance of any positive derangement of intellect, but there was a mental depression—an unaltering, invincible prostration, produced by his absolute belief in the reality of the dreadful vision that he had seen at the masked ball—which suggested to the physician the gravest doubts about the case. He saw with dismay that the patient showed no anxiety, as he got stronger, except on one subject. He was eagerly desirous of seeing Nanina every day by his bedside; but, as soon as he was assured that his wish should be faithfully complied with, he seemed to care for nothing more. Even when they proposed, in the hope of rousing him to an exhibition of something like pleasure, that the girl should read to him for an hour every day out of one of his favorite books, he only showed a languid satisfaction. Weeks passed away, and still, do what they would, they could not make him so much as smile.

One day Nanina had begun to read to him as usual, but had not proceeded far before Marta Angrisani informed her that he had fallen into a doze. She ceased with a sigh, and sat looking at him sadly, as he lay near her, faint and pale and mournful in his sleep—miserably altered from what he was when she first knew him. It had been a hard trial to watch by his bedside in the terrible time of his delirium; but it was a harder trial still to look at him now, and to feel less and less hopeful with each succeeding day.

While her eyes and thoughts were still compassionately fixed on him, the door of the bedroom opened, and the doctor came in, followed by Andrea D'Arbino, whose share in the strange adventure with the Yellow Mask caused him to feel a special interest in Fabio's progress toward recovery.

"Asleep, I see; and sighing in his sleep," said the doctor, going to the bedside. "The grand difficulty with him," he continued, turning to D'Arbino, "remains precisely what it was. I have hardly left a single means untried of rousing him from that fatal depression; yet, for the last fortnight, he has not advanced a single step. It is impossible to shake his conviction of the reality of that face which he saw (or rather which he thinks he saw) when the yellow mask was removed; and, as long as he persists in his own shocking view of the case, so long he will lie there, getting better, no doubt, as to his body, but worse as to his mind."

"I suppose, poor fellow, he is not in a fit state to be reasoned with?"

"On the contrary, like all men with a fixed delusion, he has plenty of intelligence to appeal to on every point, except the one point on which he is wrong. I have argued with him vainly by the hour together. He possesses, unfortunately, an acute nervous sensibility and a vivid imagination; and besides, he has, as I suspect, been superstitiously brought up as a child. It would be probably useless to argue rationally with him on certain spiritual subjects, even if his mind was in perfect health. He has a good deal of the mystic and the dreamer in his composition; and science and logic are but broken reeds to depend upon with men of that kind."

"Does he merely listen to you when you reason with him, or does he attempt to answer?"

"He has only one form of answer, and that is, unfortunately, the most difficult of all to dispose of. Whenever I try to convince him of his delusion, he invariably retorts by asking me for a rational explanation of what happened to him at the masked ball. Now, neither you nor I, though we believe firmly that he has been the dupe of some infamous conspiracy, have been able as yet to penetrate thoroughly into this mystery of the Yellow Mask. Our common sense tells us that he must be wrong in taking his view of it, and that we must be right in taking ours; but if we cannot give him actual, tangible proof of that—if we can only theorize, when he asks us for an explanation—it is but too plain, in his present condition, that every time we remonstrate with him on the subject we only fix him in his delusion more and more firmly."

"It is not for want of perseverance on my part," said D'Arbino, after a moment of silence, "that we are still left in the dark. Ever since the extraordinary statement of the coachman who drove the woman home, I have been inquiring and investigating. I have offered the reward of two hundred scudi for the discovery of her; I have myself examined the servants at the palace, the night-watchman at the Campo Santo, the police-books, the lists of keepers of hotels and lodging-houses, to hit on some trace of this woman; and I have failed in all directions. If my poor friend's perfect recovery does indeed depend on his delusion being combated by actual proof, I fear we have but little chance of restoring him. So far as I am concerned, I confess myself at the end of my resources."

"I hope we are not quite conquered yet," returned the doctor. "The proofs we want may turn up when we least expect them. It is certainly a miserable case," he continued, mechanically laying his fingers on the sleeping man's pulse. "There he lies, wanting nothing now but to recover the natural elasticity of his mind; and here we stand at his bedside, unable to relieve him of the weight that is pressing his faculties down. I repeat it, Signor Andrea, nothing will rouse him from his delusion that he is the victim of a supernatural interposition but the production of some startling, practical proof of his error. At present he is in the position of a man who has been imprisoned from his birth in a dark room, and who denies the existence of daylight. If we cannot open the shutters and show him the sky outside, we shall never convert him to a knowledge of the truth."

Saying these words, the doctor turned to lead the way out of the room, and observed Nanina, who had moved from the bedside on his entrance, standing near the door. He stopped to look at her, shook his head good-humoredly, and called to Marta, who happened to be occupied in an adjoining room.

"Signora Marta," said the doctor, "I think you told me some time ago that your pretty and careful little assistant lives in your house. Pray, does she take much walking exercise?"

"Very little, Signor Dottore. She goes home to her sister when she leaves the palace. Very little walking exercise, indeed."

"I thought so! Her pale cheeks and heavy eyes told me as much. Now, my dear," said the doctor, addressing Nanina, "you are a very good girl, and I am sure you will attend to what I tell you. Go out every morning before you come here, and take a walk in the fresh air. You are too young not to suffer by being shut up in close rooms every day, unless you get some regular exercise. Take a good long walk in the morning, or you will fall into my hands as a patient, and be quite unfit to continue your attendance here. Now, Signor Andrea, I am ready for you. Mind, my child, a walk every day in the open air outside the town, or you will fall ill, take my word for it!"

Nanina promised compliance; but she spoke rather absently, and seemed scarcely conscious of the kind familiarity which marked the doctor's manner. The truth was, that all her thoughts were occupied with what he had been saying by Fabio's bedside. She had not lost one word of the conversation while the doctor was talking of his patient, and of the conditions on which his recovery depended. "Oh, if that proof which would cure him could only be found!" she thought to herself, as she stole back anxiously to the bedside when the room was empty.

On getting home that day she found a letter waiting for her, and was greatly surprised to see that it was written by no less a person than the master-sculptor, Luca Lomi. It was very short; simply informing her that he had just returned to Pisa, and that he was anxious to know when she could sit to him for a new bust—a commission from a rich foreigner at Naples.

Nanina debated with herself for a moment whether she should answer the letter in the hardest way, to her, by writing, or, in the easiest way, in person; and decided on going to the studio and telling the master-sculptor that it would be impossible for her to serve him as a model, at least for some time to come. It would have taken her a long hour to say this with due propriety on paper; it would only take her a few minutes to say it with her own lips. So she put on her mantilla again and departed for the studio.

On, arriving at the gate and ringing the bell, a thought suddenly occurred to her, which she wondered had not struck her before. Was it not possible that she might meet Father Rocco in his brother's work-room? It was too late to retreat now, but not too late to ask, before she entered, if the priest was in the studio. Accordingly, when one of the workmen opened the door to her, she inquired first, very confusedly and anxiously, for Father Rocco. Hearing that he was not with his brother then, she went tranquilly enough to make her apologies to the master-sculptor.

She did not think it necessary to tell him more than that she was now occupied every day by nursing duties in a sick-room, and that it was consequently out of her power to attend at the studio. Luca Lomi expressed, and evidently felt, great disappointment at her failing him as a model, and tried hard to persuade her that she might find time enough, if she chose, to sit to him, as well as to nurse the sick person. The more she resisted his arguments and entreaties, the more obstinately he reiterated them. He was dusting his favorite busts and statues, after his long absence, with a feather-brush when she came in; and he continued this occupation all the while he was talking—urging a fresh plea to induce Nanina to reconsider her refusal to sit at every fresh piece of sculpture he came to, and always receiving the same resolute apology from her as she slowly followed him down the studio toward the door.

Arriving thus at the lower end of the room, Luca stopped with a fresh argument on his lips before his statue of Minerva. He had dusted it already, but he lovingly returned to dust it again. It was his favorite work—the only good likeness (although it did assume to represent a classical subject) of his dead daughter that he possessed. He had refused to part with it for Maddalena's sake; and, as he now approached it with his brush for the second time, he absently ceased speaking, and mounted on a stool to look at the face near and blow some specks of dust off the forehead. Nanina thought this a good opportunity of escaping from further importunities. She was on the point of slipping away to the door with a word of farewell, when a sudden exclamation from Luca Lomi arrested her.

"Plaster!" cried the master-sculptor, looking intently at that part of the hair of the statue which lay lowest on the forehead. "Plaster here!" He took out his penknife as he spoke, and removed a tiny morsel of some white substance from an interstice between two folds of the hair where it touched the face. "It *is* plaster!" he exclaimed, excitedly. "Somebody has been taking a cast from the face of my statue!"

He jumped off the stool, and looked all round the studio with an expression of suspicious inquiry. "I must have this cleared up," he said. "My statues were left under Rocco's care, and he is answerable if there has been any stealing of casts from any one of them. I must question him directly."

Nanina, seeing that he took no notice of her, felt that she might now easily effect her retreat. She opened the studio door, and repeated, for the twentieth time at least, that she was sorry she could not sit to him.

"I am sorry too, child," he said, irritably looking about for his hat. He found it apparently just as Nanina was going out; for she heard him call to one of the workmen in the inner studio, and order the man to say, if anybody wanted him, that he had gone to Father Rocco's lodgings.

VI

The next morning, when Nanina rose, a bad attack of headache, and a sense of languor and depression, reminded her of the necessity of following the doctor's advice, and preserving her health by getting a little fresh air and exercise. She had more than two hours to spare before the usual time when her daily attendance began at the Ascoli Palace; and she determined to employ the interval of leisure in taking a morning walk outside the town. La Biondella would have been glad enough to go too, but she had a large order for dinner-mats on hand, and was obliged, for that day, to stop in the house and work. Thus it happened that when Nanina set forth from home, the learned poodle, Scarammuccia, was her only companion.

She took the nearest way out of the town; the dog trotting along in his usual steady, observant way close at her side, pushing his great rough muzzle, from time to time, affectionately into her hand, and trying hard to attract her attention at intervals by barking and capering in front of her. He got but little notice, however, for his pains. Nanina was thinking again of all that the physician had said the day before by Fabio's bedside, and these thoughts brought with them others, equally absorbing, that were connected with the mysterious story of the young nobleman's adventure with the Yellow Mask. Thus preoccupied, she had little attention left for the gambols of the dog. Even the beauty of the morning appealed to her in vain. She felt the refreshment of the cool, fragrant air, but she hardly noticed the lovely blue of the sky, or the bright sunshine that gave a gayety and an interest to the commonest objects around her.

After walking nearly an hour, she began to feel tired, and looked about for a shady place to rest in.

Beyond and behind her there was only the high-road and the flat country; but by her side stood a little wooden building, half inn, half coffee-house, backed by a large, shady pleasure-garden, the gates of which stood invitingly open. Some workmen in the garden were putting up a stage for fireworks, but the place was otherwise quiet and lonely enough. It was only used at night as a sort of rustic Ranelagh, to which the citizens of Pisa resorted for pure air and amusement after the fatigues of the day. Observing that there were no visitors in the grounds, Nanina ventured in, intending to take a quarter of an hour's rest in the coolest place she could find before returning to Pisa.

She had passed the back of a wooden summer-house in a secluded part of the gardens, when she suddenly missed the dog from her side; and, looking round after him, saw that he was standing behind the summer-house with his ears erect and his nose to the ground, having evidently that instant scented something that excited his suspicion.

Thinking it possible that he might be meditating an attack on some unfortunate cat, she turned to see what he was watching. The carpenters engaged on the firework stage were just then hammering at it violently. The noise prevented her from hearing that Scarammuccia was growling, but she could feel that he was the moment she laid her hand on his back. Her curiosity was excited, and she stooped down close to him to look through a crack in the boards before which he stood into the summer-house.

She was startled at seeing a lady and gentleman sitting inside. The place she was looking through was not high enough up to enable her to see their faces, but she recognized, or thought she recognized, the pattern of the lady's dress as one which she had noticed in former days in the Demoiselle Grifoni's show-room. Rising quickly, her eye detected a hole in the boards about the level of her own height, caused by a knot having been forced out of the wood. She looked through it to ascertain, without being discovered, if the wearer of the familiar dress was the person she had taken her to be; and saw, not Brigida only, as she had expected, but Father Rocco as well. At the same moment the carpenters left off hammering and began to saw. The new sound from the firework stage was regular and not loud. The voices of the occupants of the summer-house reached her through it, and she heard Brigida pronounce the name of Count Fabio.

Instantly stooping down once more by the dog's side, she caught his muzzle firmly in both her hands. It was the only way to keep Scarammuccia from growling again, at a time when there was no din of hammering to prevent him from being heard. Those two words, "Count Fabio," in the mouth of another woman, excited a jealous anxiety in her. What could Brigida have to say in connection with that name? She never came near the Ascoli Palace—what right or reason could she have to talk of Fabio?

"Did you hear what I said?" she heard Brigida ask, in her coolest, hardest tone.

"No," the priest answered. "At least, not all of it."

"I will repeat it, then. I asked what had so suddenly determined you to give up all idea of making any future experiments on the superstitious fears of Count Fabio?"

"In the first place, the result of the experiment already tried has been so much more serious than I had anticipated, that I believe the end I had in view in making it has been answered already."

"Well; that is not your only reason?"

"Another shock to his mind might be fatal to him. I can use what I believe to be a justifiable fraud to prevent his marrying again; but I cannot burden myself with a crime."

"That is your second reason; but I believe you have another yet. The suddenness with which you sent to me last night to appoint a meeting in this lonely place; the emphatic manner in which you requested—I may almost say ordered—me to bring the wax mask here, suggest to my mind that something must have happened. What is it? I am a woman, and my curiosity must be satisfied. After the secrets you have trusted to me already, you need not hesitate, I think, to trust me with one more."

"Perhaps not. The secret this time is, moreover, of no great importance. You know that the wax mask you wore at the ball was made in a plaster mold taken off the face of my brother's statue?"

"Yes, I know that."

"My brother has just returned to his studio; has found a morsel of the plaster I used for the mold sticking in the hair of the statue; and has asked me, as the person left in charge of his work-rooms, for an explanation. Such an explanation as I could offer has not satisfied him, and he talks of making further inquiries. Considering that it will be used no more, I think it safest to destroy the wax mask, and I asked you to bring it here, that I might see it burned or broken up with my own eyes. Now you know all you wanted to know; and now, therefore, it is my turn to remind you that I have not yet had a direct answer to the first question I addressed to you when we met here. Have you brought the wax mask with you, or have you not?"

"I have not."

"And why?"

Just as that question was put, Nanina felt the dog dragging himself free of her grasp on his mouth. She had been listening hitherto with such painful intensity, with such all-absorbing emotions of suspense, terror, and astonishment, that she had not noticed his efforts to get away, and had continued mechanically to hold his mouth shut. But now she was aroused by the violence of his struggles to the knowledge that, unless she hit upon some new means of quieting him, he would have his mouth free, and would betray her by a growl.

In an agony of apprehension lest she should lose a word of the momentous conversation, she made a desperate attempt to appeal to the dog's fondness for her, by suddenly flinging both her arms round his neck, and kissing his rough, hairy cheek. The stratagem succeeded. Scarammuccia had, for many years past, never received any greater marks of his mistress's kindness for him than such as a pat on the head or a present of a lump of sugar might convey. His dog's nature was utterly confounded by the unexpected warmth of Nanina's caress, and he struggled up vigorously in her arms to try and return it by licking her face. She could easily prevent him from doing this, and could so gain a few minutes more to listen behind the summer-house without danger of discovery.

She had lost Brigida's answer to Father Rocco's question; but she was in time to hear her next words.

"We are alone here," said Brigida. "I am a woman, and I don't know that you may not have come armed. It is only the commonest precaution on my part not to give you a chance of getting at the wax mask till I have made my conditions."

"You never said a word about conditions before."

"True. I remember telling you that I wanted nothing but the novelty of going to the masquerade in the character of my dead enemy, and the luxury of being able to terrify the man who had brutally ridiculed me in old days in the studio. That was the truth. But it is not the less the truth that our experiment on Count Fabio has detained me in this city much longer than I ever intended, that I am all but penniless, and that I deserve to be paid. In plain words, will you buy the mask of me for two hundred scudi?"

"I have not twenty scudi in the world, at my own free disposal."

"You must find two hundred if you want the wax mask. I don't wish to threaten—but money I must have. I mention the sum of two hundred scudi, because that is the exact amount offered in the public handbills by Count Fabio's friends for the discovery of the woman who wore the yellow mask at the Marquis Melani's ball. What have I to do but to earn that money if I please, by going to the palace, taking the wax mask with me, and telling them that I am the woman. Suppose I confess in that way; they can do nothing to hurt me, and I should be two hundred scudi the richer. You might be injured, to be sure, if they insisted on knowing who made the wax model, and who suggested the ghastly disguise—"

"Wretch! do you believe that my character could be injured on the unsupported evidence of any words from your lips?"

"Father Rocco, for the first time since I have enjoyed the pleasure of your acquaintance, I find you committing a breach of good manners. I shall leave you until you become more like yourself. If you wish to apologize for calling me a wretch, and if you want to secure the wax mask, honor me with a visit before four o'clock this afternoon, and bring two hundred scudi with you. Delay till after four, and it will be too late."

An instant of silence followed; and then Nanina judged that Brigida must be departing, for she heard the rustling of a dress on the lawn in front of the summer-house. Unfortunately, Scarammuccia heard it too. He twisted himself round in her arms and growled.

The noise disturbed Father Rocco. She heard him rise and leave the summer-house. There would have been time enough, perhaps, for her to conceal herself among some trees if she could have recovered her self-possession at once; but she was incapable of making an effort to regain it. She could neither think nor move—her breath seemed to die away on her lips—as she saw the shadow of the priest stealing over the grass slowly from the front to the back of the summer-house. In another moment they were face to face.

He stopped a few paces from her, and eyed her steadily in dead silence. She still crouched against the summer-house, and still with one hand mechanically kept her hold of the dog. It was well for the priest that she did so. Scarammuccia's formidable teeth were in full view, his shaggy coat was bristling, his eyes were starting, his growl had changed from the surly to the savage note; he was ready to tear down, not Father Rocco only, but all the clergy in Pisa, at a moment's notice.

"You have been listening," said the priest, calmly. "I see it in your face. You have heard all."

She could not answer a word; she could not take her eyes from him. There was an unnatural stillness in his face, a steady, unrepentant, unfathomable despair in his eyes that struck her with horror. She would have given worlds to be able to rise to her feet and fly from his presence.

"I once distrusted you and watched you in secret," he said, speaking after a short silence, thoughtfully, and with a strange, tranquil sadness in his voice. "And now, what I did by you, you do by me. You put the hope of your life once in my hands. Is it because they were not worthy of the trust that discovery and ruin overtake me, and that you are the instrument of the retribution? Can this be the decree of Heaven—or is it nothing but the blind justice of chance?"

He looked upward, doubtingly, to the lustrous sky above him, and sighed. Nanina's eyes still followed his mechanically. He seemed to feel their influence, for he suddenly looked down at her again.

"What keeps you silent? Why are you afraid?" he said. "I can do you no harm, with your dog at your side, and the workmen yonder within call. I can do you no harm, and I wish to do you none. Go back to Pisa; tell what you have heard, restore the man you love to himself, and ruin me. That is your work; do it! I was never your enemy, even when I distrusted you. I am not your enemy now. It is no fault of yours that a fatality has been accomplished through you—no fault of yours that I am rejected as the instrument of securing a righteous restitution to the Church. Rise, child, and go your way, while I go mine, and prepare for what is to come. If we never meet again, remember that I parted from you without one hard saying or one harsh look—parted from you so, knowing that the first words you speak in Pisa will be death to my character, and destruction to the great purpose of my life."

Speaking these words, always with the same calmness which had marked his manner from the first, he looked fixedly at her for a little while, sighed again, and turned away. Just before he disappeared among the trees, he said "Farewell," but so softly that she could barely hear it. Some strange confusion clouded her mind as she lost sight of him. Had she injured him, or had he injured her? His words bewildered and oppressed her simple heart. Vague doubts and fears, and a sudden antipathy to remaining any longer near the summer-house, overcame her. She started to her feet, and, keeping the dog still at her side, hurried from the garden to the highroad. There, the wide glow of sunshine, the sight of the city lying before her, changed the current of her thoughts, and directed them all to Fabio and to the future.

A burning impatience to be back in Pisa now possessed her. She hastened toward the city at her utmost speed. The doctor was reported to be in the palace when she passed the servants lounging in the courtyard. He saw the moment, she came into his presence, that something had happened, and led her away from the sick-room into Fabio's empty study. There she told him all.

"You have saved him," said the doctor, joyfully. "I will answer for his recovery. Only let that woman come here for the reward; and leave me to deal with her as she deserves. In the meantime, my dear, don't go away from the palace on any account until I give you permission. I am going to send a message immediately to Signor Andrea D'Arbino to come and hear the extraordinary disclosure that you have made to me. Go back to read to the count, as usual, until I want you again; but, remember, you must not drop a word to him yet of what you have said to me. He must be carefully prepared for all that we have to tell him; and must be kept quite in the dark until those preparations are made."

D'Arbino answered the doctor's summons in person; and Nanina repeated her story to him. He and the doctor remained closeted together for some time after she had concluded her narrative and had retired. A little before four o'clock they sent for her again into the study. The doctor was sitting by the table with a bag of money before him, and D'Arbino was telling one of the servants that if a lady called at the palace on the subject of the handbill which he had circulated, she was to be admitted into the study immediately.

As the clock struck four Nanina was requested to take possession of a window-seat, and to wait there until she was summoned. When she had obeyed, the doctor loosened one of the window-curtains, to hide her from the view of any one entering the room.

About a quarter of an hour elapsed, and then the door was thrown open, and Brigida herself was shown into the study. The doctor bowed, and D'Arbino placed a chair for her. She was perfectly collected, and thanked them for their politeness with her best grace.

"I believe I am addressing confidential friends of Count Fabio d'Ascoli?" Brigida began. "May I ask if you are authorized to act for the count, in relation to the reward which this handbill offers?"

The doctor, having examined the handbill, said that the lady was quite right, and pointed significantly to the bag of money.

"You are prepared, then," pursued Brigida, smiling, "to give a reward of two hundred scudi to any one able to tell you who the woman is who wore the yellow mask at the Marquis Melani's ball, and how she contrived to personate the face and figure of the late Countess d'Ascoli?"

"Of course we are prepared," answered D'Arbino, a little irritably. "As men of honor, we are not in the habit of promising anything that we are not perfectly willing, under proper conditions, to perform."

"Pardon me, my dear friend," said the doctor; "I think you speak a little too warmly to the lady. She is quite right to take every precaution.

We have the two hundred scudi here, madam," he continued, patting the money-bag; "and we are prepared to pay that sum for the information we want. But" (here the doctor suspiciously moved the bag of scudi from the table to his lap) "we must have proofs that the person claiming the reward is really entitled to it."

Brigida's eyes followed the money-bag greedily.

"Proofs!" she exclaimed, taking a small flat box from under her cloak, and pushing it across to the doctor. "Proofs! there you will find one proof that establishes my claim beyond the possibility of doubt."

The doctor opened the box, and looked at the wax mask inside it; then handed it to D'Arbino, and replaced the bag of scudi on the table.

"The contents of that box seem certainly to explain a great deal," he said, pushing the bag gently toward Brigida, but always keeping his hand over it. "The woman who wore the yellow domino was, I presume, of the same height as the late countess?"

"Exactly," said Brigida. "Her eyes were also of the same color as the late countess's; she wore yellow of the same shade as the hangings in the late countess's room, and she had on, under her yellow mask, the colorless wax model of the late countess's face, now in your friend's hand. So much for that part of the secret. Nothing remains now to be cleared up but the mystery of who the lady was. Have the goodness, sir, to push that bag an inch or two nearer my way, and I shall be delighted to tell you."

"Thank you, madam," said the doctor, with a very perceptible change in his manner. "We know who the lady was already."

He moved the bag of scudi while he spoke back to his own side of the table. Brigida's cheeks reddened, and she rose from her seat.

"Am I to understand, sir," she said, haughtily, "that you take advantage of my position here, as a defenseless woman, to cheat me out of the reward?"

"By no means, madam," rejoined the doctor. "We have covenanted to pay the reward to the person who could give us the information we required."

"Well, sir! have I not given you part of it? And am I not prepared to give you the whole?"

"Certainly; but the misfortune is, that another person has been beforehand with you. We ascertained who the lady in the yellow domino was, and how she contrived to personate the face of the late Countess d'Ascoli, several hours ago from another informant. That person has consequently the prior claim; and, on every principle of justice, that person must also have the reward. Nanina, this bag belongs to you—come and take it."

Nanina appeared from the window-seat. Brigida, thunderstruck, looked at her in silence for a moment; gasped out, "That girl!"—then stopped again, breathless.

"That girl was at the back of the summer-house this morning, while you and your accomplice were talking together," said the doctor.

D'Arbino had been watching Brigida's face intently from the moment of Nanina's appearance, and had quietly stolen close to her side. This was a fortunate movement; for the doctor's last words were hardly out of his mouth before Brigida seized a heavy ruler lying, with some writing materials, on the table. In another instant, if D'Arbino had not caught her arm, she would have hurled it at Nanina's head.

"You may let go your hold, sir," she said, dropping the ruler, and turning toward D'Arbino with a smile on her white lips and a wicked calmness in her steady eyes. "I can wait for a better opportunity."

With those words she walked to the door; and, turning round there, regarded Nanina fixedly.

"I wish I had been a moment quicker with the ruler," she said, and went out.

"There!" exclaimed the doctor; "I told you I knew how to deal with her as she deserved. One thing I am certainly obliged to her for—she has saved us the trouble of going to her house and forcing her to give up the mask. And now, my child," he continued, addressing Nanina, "you can go home, and one of the men-servants shall see you safe to your own door, in case that woman should still be lurking about the palace. Stop! you are leaving the bag of scudi behind you."

"I can't take it, sir."

"And why not?"

"*She* would have taken money!" Saying those words, Nanina reddened, and looked toward the door.

The doctor glanced approvingly at D'Arbino. "Well, well, we won't argue about that now," he said. "I will lock up the money with the mask for to-day. Come here to-morrow morning as usual, my dear. By that time I shall have made up my mind on the right means for breaking your discovery to Count Fabio. Only let us proceed slowly and cautiously, and I answer for success."

VII

The next morning, among the first visitors at the Ascoli Palace was the master-sculptor, Luca Lomi. He seemed, as the servants thought, agitated, and said he was especially desirous of seeing Count Fabio. On being informed that this was impossible, he reflected a little, and then inquired if the medical attendant of the count was at the palace, and could be spoken with. Both questions were answered in the affirmative, and he was ushered into the doctor's presence.

"I know not how to preface what I want to say," Luca began, looking about him confusedly. "May I ask you, in the first place, if the work-girl named Nanina was here yesterday?"

"She was," said the doctor.

"Did she speak in private with any one?"

"Yes; with me."

"Then you know everything?"

"Absolutely everything."

"I am glad at least to find that my object in wishing to see the count can be equally well answered by seeing you. My brother, I regret to say—" He stopped perplexedly, and drew from his pocket a roll of papers.

"You may speak of your brother in the plainest terms," said the doctor. "I know what share he has had in promoting the infamous conspiracy of the Yellow Mask."

"My petition to you, and through you to the count, is, that your knowledge of what my brother has done may go no further. If this scandal becomes public it will ruin me in my profession. And I make little enough by it already," said Luca, with his old sordid smile breaking out again faintly on his face.

"Pray do you come from your brother with this petition?" inquired the doctor.

"No; I come solely on my own account. My brother seems careless what happens. He has made a full statement of his share in the matter from the first; has forwarded it to his ecclesiastical superior (who will send it to the archbishop), and is now awaiting whatever sentence they choose to pass on him. I have a copy of the document, to prove that he has at least been candid, and that he does not shrink from consequences which he might have avoided by flight. The law cannot touch him, but the Church can—and to the Church he has confessed. All I ask is, that he may be spared a public exposure. Such an exposure would do no good to the count, and it would do dreadful injury to me. Look over the papers yourself, and show them, whenever you think proper, to the master of this house. I have every confidence in his honor and kindness, and in yours."

He laid the roll of papers open on the table, and then retired with great humility to the window. The doctor looked over them with some curiosity.

The statement or confession began by boldly avowing the writer's conviction that part of the property which the Count Fabio d'Ascoli had inherited from his ancestors had been obtained by fraud and misrepresentation from the Church. The various authorities on which this assertion was based were then produced in due order; along with some curious particles of evidence culled from old manuscripts, which it must have cost much trouble to collect and decipher.

The second section was devoted, at great length, to the reasons which induced the writer to think it his absolute duty, as an affectionate son and faithful servant of the Church, not to rest until he had restored to the successors of the apostles in his day the property which had been fraudulently taken from them in days gone by. The writer held himself justified, in the last resort, and in that only, in using any means for effecting this restoration, except such as might involve him in mortal sin.

The third section described the priest's share in promoting the marriage of Maddalena Lomi with Fabio; and the hopes he entertained of securing the restitution of the Church property through his influence over his niece, in the first place, and, when she had died, through his influence over her child, in the second. The necessary failure of all his projects, if Fabio married again, was next glanced at; and the time at which the first suspicion of the possible occurrence of this catastrophe occurred to his mind was noted with scrupulous accuracy.

The fourth section narrated the manner in which the conspiracy of the Yellow Mask had originated. The writer described himself as being in his brother's studio on the night of his niece's death, harassed by forebodings of the likelihood of Fabio's marrying again, and filled with the resolution to prevent any such disastrous second union at all hazards. He asserted that the idea of taking the wax mask from his brother's statue flashed upon him on a sudden, and that he knew of nothing to lead to it, except, perhaps, that he had been thinking just before of the superstitious nature of the young man's character, as he had himself observed it in the studio. He further declared that the idea of the wax mask terrified him at first; that he strove against it as against a temptation of the devil; that, from fear of yielding to this temptation, he abstained even from entering the studio during his brother's absence at Naples, and that he first faltered in his good resolution when Fabio returned to Pisa, and when it was rumored, not only that the young nobleman was going to the ball, but that he would certainly marry for the second time.

The fifth section related that the writer, upon this, yielded to temptation rather than forego the cherished purpose of his life by allowing Fabio a chance of marrying again—that he made the wax mask in a plaster mold taken from the face of his brother's statue—and that he then had two separate interviews with a woman named Brigida (of whom he had some previous knowledge), who was ready and anxious, from motives of private malice, to personate the deceased countess at the masquerade. This woman had suggested that some anonymous letters to Fabio would pave the way in his mind for the approaching impersonation, and had written the letters herself. However, even when all the preparations were made, the writer declared that he shrank from proceeding to extremities; and that he would have abandoned the whole project but for the woman Brigida informing him one day that a work-girl named Nanina was to be one of the attendants at the ball. He knew the count to have been in love with this girl, even to the point of wishing to marry her; he suspected that her engagement to wait at the ball was preconcerted; and, in consequence, he authorized his female accomplice to perform her part in the conspiracy.

The sixth section detailed the proceedings at the masquerade, and contained the writer's confession that, on the night before it, he had written to the count proposing the reconciliation of a difference that had taken place between them, solely for the purpose of guarding himself against suspicion. He next acknowledged that he had borrowed the key of the Campo Santo gate, keeping the authority to whom it was intrusted in perfect ignorance of the purpose for which he wanted it. That purpose was to carry out the ghastly delusion of the wax mask (in the very probable event of the wearer being followed and inquired after) by having the woman Brigida taken up and set down at the gate of the cemetery in which Fabio's wife had been buried.

The seventh section solemnly averred that the sole object of the conspiracy was to prevent the young nobleman from marrying again, by working on his superstitious fears; the writer repeating, after this avowal, that any such second marriage would necessarily destroy his project for promoting the ultimate restoration of the Church possessions, by diverting Count Fabio's property, in great part, from his first wife's child, over whom the priest would always have influence, to another wife and probably other children, over whom he could hope to have none.

The eighth and last section expressed the writer's contrition for having allowed his zeal for the Church to mislead him into actions liable to bring scandal on his cloth; reiterated in the strongest language his conviction that, whatever might be thought of the means employed, the end he had proposed to himself was a most righteous one; and concluded by asserting his resolution to suffer with humility any penalties, however severe, which his ecclesiastical superiors might think fit to inflict on him.

Having looked over this extraordinary statement, the doctor addressed himself again to Luca Lomi.

"I agree with you," he said, "that no useful end is to be gained now by mentioning your brother's conduct in public—always provided, however, that his ecclesiastical superiors do their duty. I shall show these papers to the count as soon as he is fit to peruse them, and I have no doubt that he will be ready to take my view of the matter."

This assurance relieved Luca Lomi of a great weight of anxiety. He bowed and withdrew.

The doctor placed the papers in the same cabinet in which he had secured the wax mask. Before he locked the doors again he took out the flat box, opened it, and looked thoughtfully for a few minutes at the mask inside, then sent for Nanina.

"Now, my child," he said, when she appeared, "I am going to try our first experiment with Count Fabio; and I think it of great importance that you should be present while I speak to him."

He took up the box with the mask in it, and beckoning to Nanina to follow him, led the way to Fabio's chamber.

VIII

A bout six months after the events already related, Signor Andrea D'Arbino and the Cavaliere Finello happened to be staying with a friend, in a seaside villa on the Castellamare shore of the bay of Naples. Most of their time was pleasantly occupied on the sea, in fishing and sailing. A boat was placed entirely at their disposal. Sometimes they loitered whole days along the shore; sometimes made trips to the lovely islands in the bay.

One evening they were sailing near Sorrento, with a light wind. The beauty of the coast tempted them to keep the boat close inshore. A short time before sunset, they rounded the most picturesque headland they had yet passed; and a little bay, with a white-sand beach, opened on their view. They noticed first a villa surrounded by orange and olive trees on the rocky heights inland; then a path in the cliff-side leading down to the sands; then a little family party on the beach, enjoying the fragrant evening air.

The elders of the group were a lady and gentleman, sitting together on the sand. The lady had a guitar in her lap and was playing a simple dance melody. Close at her side a young child was rolling on the beach in high glee; in front of her a little girl was dancing to the music, with a very extraordinary partner in the shape of a dog, who was capering on his hind legs in the most grotesque manner. The merry laughter of the girl, and the lively notes of the guitar were heard distinctly across the still water.

"Edge a little nearer in shore," said D'Arbino to his friend, who was steering; "and keep as I do in the shadow of the sail. I want to see the faces of those persons on the beach without being seen by them."

Finello obeyed. After approaching just near enough to see the countenances of the party on shore, and to be barked at lustily by the dog, they turned the boat's head again toward the offing.

"A pleasant voyage, gentlemen," cried the clear voice of the little girl. They waved their hats in return; and then saw her run to the dog and take him by the forelegs. "Play, Nanina," they heard her say. "I have not half done with my partner yet." The guitar sounded once more, and the grotesque dog was on his hind legs in a moment.

"I had heard that he was well again, that he had married her lately, and that he was away with her and her sister, and his child by the first wife,"

WILKIE COLLINS

said D'Arbino; "but I had no suspicion that their place of retirement was so near us. It is too soon to break in upon their happiness, or I should have felt inclined to run the boat on shore."

"I never heard the end of that strange adventure of the Yellow Mask," said Finello. "There was a priest mixed up in it, was there not?"

"Yes; but nobody seems to know exactly what has become of him. He was sent for to Rome, and has never been heard of since. One report is, that he has been condemned to some mysterious penal seclusion by his ecclesiastical superiors—another, that he has volunteered, as a sort of Forlorn Hope, to accept a colonial curacy among rough people, and in a pestilential climate. I asked his brother, the sculptor, about him a little while ago, but he only shook his head, and said nothing."

"And the woman who wore the yellow mask?"

"She, too, has ended mysteriously. At Pisa she was obliged to sell off everything she possessed to pay her debts. Some friends of hers at a milliner's shop, to whom she applied for help, would have nothing to do with her. She left the city, alone and penniless."

The boat had approached the next headland on the coast while they were talking. They looked back for a last glance at the beach. Still the notes of the guitar came gently across the quiet water; but there mingled with them now the sound of the lady's voice. She was singing. The little girl and the dog were at her feet, and the gentleman was still in his old place close at her side.

In a few minutes more the boat rounded the next headland, the beach vanished from view, and the music died away softly in the distance.

LAST LEAVES FROM LEAH'S DIARY

3d of June

Our stories are ended; our pleasant work is done. It is a lovely summer afternoon. The great hall at the farmhouse, after having been filled with people, is now quite deserted. I sit alone at my little work-table, with rather a crying sensation at my heart, and with the pen trembling in my fingers, as if I was an old woman already. Our manuscript has been sealed up and taken away; the one precious object of all our most anxious thoughts for months past—our third child, as we have got to call it—has gone out from us on this summer's day, to seek its fortune in the world.

A little before twelve o'clock last night, my husband dictated to me the last words of "The Yellow Mask." I laid down the pen, and closed the paper thoughtfully. With that simple action the work that we had wrought at together so carefully and so long came to a close. We were both so silent and still, that the murmuring of the trees in the night air sounded audibly and solemnly in our room.

William's collection of stories has not, thus far, been half exhausted yet; but those who understand the public taste and the interests of bookselling better than we, think it advisable not to risk offering too much to the reader at first. If individual opinions can be accepted as a fair test, our prospects of success seem hopeful. The doctor (but we must not forget that he is a friend) was so pleased with the two specimen stories we sent to him, that he took them at once to his friend, the editor of the newspaper, who showed his appreciation of what he read in a very gratifying manner. He proposed that William should publish in the newspaper, on very fair terms, any short anecdotes and curious experiences of his life as a portrait-painter, which might not be important enough to put into a book. The money which my husband has gained from time to time in this way has just sufficed to pay our expenses at the farmhouse up to within the last month; and now our excellent friends here say they will not hear anything more from us on the subject of the rent until the book is sold and we have plenty of money. This is one great relief and happiness. Another, for which I feel even more grateful, is that William's eyes have gained so much by their long rest, that even the doctor is surprised at the progress he has made. He only puts on his green shade now when he goes out into the sun, or when the candles are lit. His spirits are infinitely raised, and he is beginning to talk already of the time when he will unpack his palette and brushes, and take to his old portrait-painting occupations again.

With all these reasons for being happy, it seems unreasonable and ungracious in me to be feeling sad, as I do just at this moment. I can only say, in my own justification, that it is a mournful ceremony to take leave of an old friend; and I have taken leave twice over of the book that has been like an old friend to me—once when I had written the last word in it, and once again when I saw it carried away to London.

I packed the manuscript up with my own hands this morning, in thick brown paper, wasting a great deal of sealing-wax, I am afraid, in my anxiety to keep the parcel from bursting open in case it should be knocked about on its journey to town. Oh me, how cheap and common it looked, in its new form, as I carried it downstairs! A dozen pairs of worsted stockings would have made a larger parcel; and half a crown's worth of groceries would have weighed a great deal heavier.

Just as we had done dinner the doctor and the editor came in. The first had called to fetch the parcel—I mean the manuscript; the second had come out with him to Appletreewick for a walk. As soon as the farmer heard that the book was to be sent to London, he insisted that we should drink success to it all round. The children, in high glee, were mounted up on the table, with a glass of currant-wine apiece; the rest of us had ale; the farmer proposed the toast, and his sailor son led the cheers. We all joined in (the children included), except the editor—who, being the only important person of the party, could not, I suppose, afford to compromise his dignity by making a noise. He was extremely polite, however, in a lofty way, to me, waving his hand and bowing magnificently every time he spoke. This discomposed me a little; and I was still more flurried when he said that he had written to the London publishers that very day, to prepare them for the arrival of our book.

"Do you think they will print it, sir?" I ventured to ask.

"My dear madam, you may consider it settled," said the editor, confidently. "The letter is written—the thing is done. Look upon the book as published already; pray oblige me by looking upon the book as published already."

"Then the only uncertainty now is about how the public will receive it!" said my husband, fidgeting in his chair, and looking nervously at me.

"Just so, my dear sir, just so," answered the editor. "Everything depends upon the public—everything, I pledge you my word of honor."

"Don't look doubtful, Mrs. Kerby; there isn't a doubt about it," whispered the kind doctor, giving the manuscript a confident smack as he passed by me with it on his way to the door.

In another minute he and the editor, and the poor cheap-looking brown paper parcel, were gone. The others followed them out, and I was left in the hall alone.

Oh, Public! Public! it all depends now upon you! The children are to have new clothes from top to toe; I am to have a black silk gown; William is to buy a beautiful traveling color-box; the rent is to be paid; all our kind friends at the farmhouse are to have little presents, and our future way in this hard world is to be smoothed for us at the outset, if you will only accept a poor painter's stories which his wife has written down for him After Dark!

A Note About the Author

Wilkie Collins (1824–1889) was an English novelist and playwright. Born in London, Collins was raised in England, Italy, and France by William Collins, a renowned landscape painter, and his wife Harriet Geddes. After working for a short time as a tea merchant, he published *Antonina* (1850), his literary debut. He quickly became known as a leading author of sensation novels, a popular genre now recognized as a forerunner to detective fiction. Encouraged on by the success of his early work, Collins made a name for himself on the London literary scene. He soon befriended Charles Dickens, forming a strong bond grounded in friendship and mentorship that would last several decades. His novels *The Woman in White* (1859) and *The Moonstone* (1868) are considered pioneering examples of mystery and detective fiction, and enabled Collins to become financially secure. Toward the end of the 1860s, at the height of his career, Collins began to suffer from numerous illnesses, including gout and opium addiction, which contributed to his decline as a writer. Beyond his literary work, Collins is seen as an early advocate for marriage reform, criticizing the institution and living a radically open romantic lifestyle.

A Note from the Publisher

Spanning many genres, from non-fiction essays to literature classics to children's books and lyric poetry, Mint Edition books showcase the master works of our time in a modern new package. The text is freshly typeset, is clean and easy to read, and features a new note about the author in each volume. Many books also include exclusive new introductory material. Every book boasts a striking new cover, which makes it as appropriate for collecting as it is for gift giving. Mint Edition books are only printed when a reader orders them, so natural resources are not wasted. We're proud that our books are never manufactured in excess and exist only in the exact quantity they need to be read and enjoyed.

bookfinity™

Discover more of your favorite classics with Bookfinity™.

- Track your reading with custom book lists.
- Get great book recommendations for your personalized Reader Type.
- Add reviews for your favorite books.
- AND MUCH MORE!

Visit **bookfinity.com** and take the fun Reader Type quiz to get started.

Enjoy our classic and modern companion pairings!

Printed in the USA
CPSIA information can be obtained
at www.ICGtesting.com
JSHW082147140824
68134JS00002B/15